"*Carrie said we should try to be friends again,*"

Emma said.

"Easier said than done," Kurt pointed out. "I mean, how do we go back to that after everything that's happened?"

"I don't know," Emma admitted.

"I'll tell you, it's rough," Kurt said. "My dad is glad to see me, of course, but there's all this pressure from him to never see you again—"

"He hates me—"

"He just doesn't want to see me get hurt again," Kurt said. "You can understand that."

"Well, my parents don't want to see me get hurt again, either," Emma said defensively. "It works both ways, you know."

D0595185

The SUNSET ISLAND series
by Cherie Bennett

The CLUB SUNSET ISLAND series
by Cherie Bennett

Also created by Cherie Bennett

Sunset Fire

CHERIE BENNETT

Sunset™ Island

SPLASH™

A BERKLEY / SPLASH BOOK

SUNSET FIRE is an original publication of
The Berkley Publishing Group.
This work has never appeared before in book form.

SUNSET FIRE

A Berkley Book / published by arrangement with
General Licensing Company, Inc.

PRINTING HISTORY
Berkley edition / September 1994

A GLC BOOK

Splash and *Sunset Island* are trademarks belonging to
General Licensing Company, Inc.

ISBN: 0-425-14360-0

BERKLEY®
Berkley Books are published by
The Berkley Publishing Group,
200 Madison Avenue, New York, New York 10016.
BERKLEY and the "B" design
are trademarks belonging to Berkley Publishing Corporation.

PRINTED IN THE UNITED STATES OF AMERICA

10 9 8 7 6 5 4 3 2 1

For my tender guy

ONE

"These animals are unbelievably cute," Emma Cresswell said as she and her two best friends, Samantha "Sam" Bridges and Carrie Alden, walked through the animal shelter. Emma's hand was entwined with that of five-year-old Katie Hewitt, and Katie was oohing and aahing over every cat and dog she saw.

"Hey, let's find some real mangy-looking female dog who's in heat and name her Diana," Sam quipped. She was referring to Diana De Witt, the girls' archenemy, a witch to end all witches.

"But I can't get a dog," Katie said solemnly, staring with round eyes at Sam.

1

"My parents said I can only get a cat." She looked up at Emma. "I miss Dog."

Emma knelt down and hugged the little girl. The week before, the Hewitt family's beloved pooch, cleverly named Dog, had to be put to sleep because of inoperable cancer. "I know you do, sweetie," Emma said soothingly. "I miss Dog, too."

"Did he go to heaven?" Katie asked.

"I think so," Emma said. She traded looks with Sam, who just rolled her eyes. Sam was not a big believer in the great hereafter.

"Don't those basset hound's eyes look kind of like Billy's?" Carrie asked with a sigh.

"Carrie babe, you've been without your guy entirely too long," Sam told her. "That basset hound is slobbering. Billy doesn't slobber."

Billy Sampson was Carrie's boyfriend, who had recently gone home to his family in Seattle after his dad was in a serious accident. Carrie missed him terribly, and no one—Billy included—knew when he'd be able to return to beautiful Sunset Island off the coast of Maine.

"There are a lot of kittens over here," Emma told Katie, leading the little girl down the aisle. The kittens yelped and mewed, tumbling over one another. "Do you see one you like?"

Katie peered into the cage. "I like them all."

"They are really cute," Sam agreed, shaking her wild red hair over her shoulders. She stuck a pinky into the cage and a little white kitten licked her finger. "Why aren't human babies this cute?"

"Some people think they are," Emma told her.

"I doubt it," Sam snorted. "Besides, show me a human baby you can leave for a couple of days with some food, water, and a litter box, and I'll show you a cute human baby."

"Something tells me Sam isn't ready for motherhood," Carrie told Emma with a laugh.

"Who is?" Emma asked with a shrug.

"Can I get two kitties?" Katie asked.

"No, sweetie," Emma replied. "Your parents said one."

Katie thought for a moment. "How about if I get one and you get one?"

Emma laughed. "Well, since I live at your house and spend my time taking care of you, it would be just the same as if you had two, wouldn't it?"

Katie thought again. "What if you gave one to Kurt? Then it could live at Kurt's house, but I could come visit it!"

Emma smiled. Her long-time boyfriend, Kurt Ackerman, had just recently returned to the island. Only now he was very much her *ex*-boyfriend. He and Emma had come close to getting married, and then . . . Emma shuddered. *I hate to even think about it,* she admitted to herself. *But now he's back, and maybe, just maybe, we have a second chance. And then again, maybe I'm a hopeless dreamer.*

"So, what do you think?" Katie prodded Emma. "That's a good idea, isn't it?"

"I don't think so," Emma said gently.

"You're glad Kurt's back, aren't you?" Katie asked her.

Sam laughed. "This kid knows everything that goes on on this island!"

"Let's pick out a kitty," Emma said, deftly changing the subject.

Katie peered into the cage. "Can I hold the white one?"

Emma opened the cage and took out the tiny all-white kitten. She put it in Katie's arms, and it immediately curled up and fell asleep.

"Oh, it's so sweet!" Katie cried, stroking the kitten's white fur.

"It really is," Carrie agreed, petting the tiny creature.

"Hey, look at this guy!" Sam said, pointing to the cage. A black-and-white kitten even smaller than the white one was batting the edge of the cage with his paw. "He's hilarious! He thinks he's a big tough guy!"

Sam lifted the black and white kitten out of the cage and held it up to her face. His nose was black, as if he had dipped it in ink. "Hey there, little fella!"

"You sure it's a guy?" Carrie asked.

Sam lifted the animal and looked underneath. "I think so." The kitten immediately batted her in the nose and mewed, and Sam laughed. "I love this cat!"

"I love this one," Katie said, snuggling against the white kitten.

"But that one is boring," Sam pointed out. "Don't you want a fun cat with personality like Bubba here?"

"Bubba?" Carrie echoed.

Sam shrugged. "He looks like a Bubba. He fights first and ask questions later." The kitten hit Sam in the nose again. "Oh, so you want to get tough, do you?" She nuzzled her nose against his nose and he began to purr. "I'm in love," Sam sighed.

"Name him Pres, then," Carrie suggested. Pres was Sam's boyfriend, a darling guy with the cutest Tennessee twang to his voice.

"This is my kitten," Katie decided, holding the white furball close. "I'm going to call her Snow White."

"Great," Emma told her. "Let's take her

6

up to the front and find out what we have to do so that you can adopt her." She turned to Sam. "Time to put Bubba back in the cage."

Sam sighed and kissed Bubba on the nose. "Bye, big boy. It's been swell." As Sam was putting the kitten back into the cage, it put its claws into her T-shirt and held on for dear life. "He doesn't want to let go!"

"You just have a way with guys," Carrie teased her.

Sam pulled Bubba's claws out of her T-shirt. She held him up at eye level. "You don't want to go back into the crowded, icky cage, do you?" Sam asked Bubba. She shook the cat back and forth so it looked as if Bubba were shaking his head no. "See? How can I put him back?" she asked her friends.

"But what would Dan Jacobs say if you got a kitten?" Carrie asked practically.

Sam was the au pair for Dan Jacobs's fourteen-year-old twin daughters, Allie and Becky Jacobs. They were really too old to need a babysitter, but Dan had hired Sam to act as sort of big sister/role model for the twins, since he was raising them solo.

"I have no idea," Sam said. She kissed Bubba on the nose. "But I have a feeling I'm going to find out!"

"You're getting a kitty, too?" Katie asked with excitement.

"Yeah," Sam decided. "I am."

"Hey, maybe Snow White and Bubba can have play dates like me and Chloe!" Katie suggested eagerly, referring to Chloe Templeton, Carrie's five-year-old charge. Everyone laughed as they walked to the front office to officially adopt their new pets.

"I love you already," Katie told Snow White. "You're going to meet all my friends, like Chloe and Stinky Stein—he lives next door—and Kurt Ackerman who taught me to swim. . . ."

Kurt Ackerman. Emma sighed just at the mention of his name. As the young girl behind the counter filled out the paperwork on the animals, Emma's mind wandered. She had a date with Kurt planned for that night. *And frankly, I'm really nervous,* she admitted to herself. *I don't know how to be with him anymore. We can't be like we used to be, back before we broke up and he left the island because I had hurt him so badly. And I don't think we can pretend all that never happened, either.*

Emma glanced over at Carrie and Sam, who were playing with Bubba. Emma smiled. *I am so lucky to have the two of them as my best friends,* she thought. *They helped me get through all the pain over Kurt. They're always there for me.*

"Listen, Bubba," Sam was saying, "we gotta talk about the birds and the bees, you know what I'm saying? I know Snow White over there is quite the babe, but surely you're not planning on getting romantically involved—"

"Sam, Bubba is only about ten weeks old," Carrie said.

"Well, it's never to early to educate," Sam said, giving Bubba a stern look.

Emma laughed. *It's so funny,* she thought, *because Sam, Carrie, and I are so different from one another. If we hadn't all gotten jobs as au pairs on Sunset Island, we never would have met. Sam is a tall, thin redhead from tiny Junction, Kansas, who wishes she was rich and famous; brown-haired, girl-next-door Carrie goes to Yale and is the smartest girl I know, and I'm . . .* Emma sighed. *What am I, anyway? Well, I'm blond and petite and the truth is I'm a rich heiress, though I try not to let people know that. But what else? Well, I guess that's what I'm trying to figure out. . . .*

"Miss? You'll need to bring the cat in for her shots in six weeks," the girl behind the counter said, getting Emma's attention.

"All right," Emma agreed.

Katie made a face. "I hate shots and so does Snow White."

"This shot will make sure Snow White doesn't get sick," the girl behind the counter told Katie. She looked back at Emma. "Also, when Snow White is about ten months old, you'll want to bring her back to be spayed."

"What's that?" Katie asked.

"They give her an operation so that she won't have kittens," Emma explained.

"But what if she wants to marry Bubba?" Katie asked.

"Bubba's gonna be a busy bee who plans to pollinate many flowers," Sam intoned.

"Bubba has to come in to get neutered," the girl behind the counter said patiently.

"Poor Bubba," Sam sighed.

Sam and Emma got some kitten food and some litter and left a donation, then they put the kittens in their new portable cardboard carrying cases and walked outside into the Maine sunshine.

"I hope you did the right thing," Carrie told Sam, reaching into her purse for her sunglasses. "I mean, what are you going to do if Dan doesn't let you keep Bubba?"

"He has to," Sam said. "I can't desert Bubba now, he's mine. We belong to each other." Bubba mewed from inside his box. "I gotta boogie—the twins are getting home early from camp today for some reason or other. I'll call you guys later, okay?"

"Sure," Carrie said. She and Emma had

come together in the Hewitts' car, so she walked in the opposite direction from Sam.

"Oh, hey," Sam called from across the parking lot, turning back to her friends, "good luck with Kurt tonight!"

"Thanks," Emma called back. "I'll need it."

"Not you, Ice Princess!" Sam called. "You've got it under control!" She gave Emma the thumbs-up sign and slid Bubba's box into the car.

Emma, Katie, and Carrie got into the Hewitts' BMW.

"Snow White fell asleep," Katie reported, peering into the box.

"A nice, docile cat, that's what we like to see," Emma murmured, starting up the car.

"Are you nervous about tonight?" Carrie asked Emma.

"Yes," Emma admitted. "Very."

"I envy you," Carrie said with a sigh. She stared out the window as Emma pulled out onto Shore Road. "I miss Billy so much."

"Have you heard from him lately?" Emma asked.

"He calls me almost every night," Carrie reported. "His dad is somewhat better— well, I guess I told you that the other day. But the doctors say it may be a really long time before he can go back to work. Meanwhile Billy is running his dad's auto shop."

"Does Billy have any interest in cars?" Emma asked, stopping at a red light.

"No," Carrie said bluntly. "But he feels like it's his responsibility to stay there until . . . until I don't know when!"

"I really believe it's going to work out for the two of you," Emma said firmly. "You've always had a saner, healthier relationship with Billy than I've had with Kurt—or Sam has had with Pres, for that matter!"

"I just wish I knew when he's coming back," Carrie said glumly. "It's so hard . . . and he keeps pressing me to come to Seattle."

"For how long?" Emma asked.

Carrie shrugged. "That part is never quite clear." Carrie sighed again. "Let's talk about you and Kurt—this subject is too depressing."

"I love Kurt," Katie piped up from the backseat.

Emma smiled. "I know you do, sweetie."

"I think you should marry him," Katie said. "Then I could be a flower girl for real."

"I don't think so," Emma replied. "I'm not ready to get married."

"Me, either," Katie agreed. She stuck her finger into the small hole in the cat carrier. "And now that Snow White is going to have an operation where she can't have babies, she won't be ready to get married, either!"

Carrie laughed. "That may be logical, somehow or other." She turned back to Emma. "Listen, just remember that you and Kurt were friends first. Maybe you can start by being friends again. Anyway, now you guys need to take it slow."

"I know that," Emma agreed. She turned the car up the Templetons' long private drive. "But I don't know what Kurt wants, or what he expects. And I guess I don't know what I want, either." She stopped the car in front of the Templetons' sprawling home and turned off the motor.

"It's okay not to know," Carrie said gently.

"That's what I keep telling myself," Emma said with a wry smile.

Carrie got out of the car and stuck her head back in the window. "Do you and Snow White want to get in the front with Emma?" she asked Katie.

"Snow White is sleeping," Katie whispered. "I don't want to move her."

"Okay," Carrie whispered. "Enjoy your new kitty." She turned to Emma. "Call me when you get back tonight if you want. I'll be up late watching horror movies with Ian—I promised him a triple-horror-movie marathon."

"Gee, sounds swell," Emma said with a laugh. "Enjoy the blood and gore!" She started up the car and pulled it down the driveway.

"Emma?" came Katie's voice from the backseat.

"What, sweetie?"

"Do you love Kurt?"

This child is certainly direct, Emma thought ruefully. "Yes, I do," she finally replied.

"So, if you love him, how come you didn't marry him?" Katie asked.

"Well, you can love someone and not be ready to get married," Emma explained.

"Why aren't you ready?"

"I'm only nineteen," Emma explained patiently. "And I think that Kurt and I have some issues to work out between us, too. He has a big problem with the fact that I'm rich, and he got too possessive and—" All of a sudden Emma realized she was confiding in a five-year-old child. "We just have a lot of talking to do," she finished lamely.

"And kissing?" Katie asked, sounding hopeful. She was very into romance and kissing these days. "Will you guys be kissing?"

Emma gave a small laugh. "Katie, my

dear," she said, "that is a question to which I honestly do not know the answer."

But I'm going to find out, Emma added to herself. I'm going to find out very, very soon.

TWO

Ding-dong. The front doorbell of the Hewitts' house rang. It was seven o'clock that evening, and Emma was in the kitchen talking with her employer, Jane Hewitt. When she heard the bell, her heart beat double-time in her chest. She knew it was Kurt.

So did Katie. Before Emma could even get up from the kitchen table, she heard Katie running from the family room into the front hall to get the door. "It has to be Kurt!" she yelled.

"I think she's more excited than I am," Emma told Jane.

Jane raised her eyebrows at Emma and

smiled. "I doubt it," she said. "She just doesn't hide it as well."

Emma blushed. "Excuse me," she said, and with a deep breath she headed into the front hall.

"Kurt!" Katie squealed, running toward the object of her affection. She jumped up and threw herself into his arms. "I missed you!"

Kurt kissed the little girl on the cheek, hugged her tight, and then set her down. "I missed you, too," he told her. As he straightened up, he took in Emma, standing a few feet away from him.

I hope I wore the right thing, Emma thought self-consciously. *I've never changed my outfit so many times in my life.*

She had finally decided on a simple white baby-doll dress with tiny yellow daisies sprinkled across the hem. She wore white sandals and tiny white pearl earrings. She'd sprayed herself liberally with the deliciously fresh Sunset Magic perfume, but she'd kept her makeup to a minimum—mascara, a thin smudged line of eyeliner, lip gloss, and to enhance her tan, the tiniest brush of peach blush across her cheekbones.

At the moment, though, she could feel her cheeks burning. *Well, I guess I didn't really need that blush for color after all,* she thought ironically.

"Doesn't Emma look pretty?" Katie prompted Kurt, grabbing his hand and holding it tight.

"Yes, she does," Kurt said, not taking his eyes off Emma.

"And doesn't Kurt look handsome?" Katie asked Emma eagerly, grabbing on to her hand. Kurt had on jeans and a blue and white striped rugby shirt.

"Yes, he does," Emma replied in a low voice. *I remember that shirt,* she thought. *The sky-blue stripes match his eyes. . . .*

Katie looked seriously from Emma to Kurt and back to Emma again. "You guys can kiss now if you want."

Kurt laughed uncomfortably. "Hey, how's your swimming coming?" he asked the little girl, obviously wanting to change the subject.

"It was better when you were teaching me," Katie replied. "Hey, Dog died and I got a new kitty and her name is Snow White. Want to meet her?"

"Sure," Kurt agreed.

"I'll get her. You stay here," Katie instructed before dashing off.

Kurt stuck his hands in the pockets of his jeans. "She's a great little girl."

"Yes, she certainly is," Emma agreed, knowing that she sounded hopelessly formal, but not feeling as if she could do anything about it.

"So . . . Dog died, huh?" Kurt asked.

"Actually he was very sick, so he had to be put to sleep," Emma explained.

"Too bad," Kurt said.

They both stared at each other. The silence was awkward and it felt as if it went on forever.

"Hi," thirteen-year-old Ethan said, coming into the hall from the family room, where he'd been watching a video.

Emma breathed a sigh of relief. She'd never been so glad to see Ethan in her life.

"Hi, Ethan, how's it going?" Kurt said, shaking Ethan's hand.

Ethan shrugged and leaned against the wall. "Dog died, ya know."

"Katie told me," Kurt said. "I'm sorry."

"It really stinks, if you ask me," Ethan said. "And that expression—'put him to sleep'—that is so lame. We killed him, us and the vet. That's what it really was."

"It was just so Dog wouldn't suffer," Emma told Ethan gently.

"Yeah, that's what everyone keeps saying," Ethan replied in a dubious tone of voice. "But what if I were sick or something? Would someone just, like, put me to sleep?"

"You're a person," Emma said.

"So?" Ethan asked. "Dog was a member of this family, just like me. At least *I* thought he was."

"Here's Snow White," Katie cried, running downstairs with the tiny ball of white fur. "Isn't she the most beautiful kitty ever?" She held the kitten up for Kurt to see.

"Gorgeous," Kurt agreed.

"You better just hope she never gets sick," Ethan said darkly. "That's all I have to say. See ya," he added to Kurt, and shuffled back into the family room.

"I gotta take Snow White back to bed," Katie said. "She's very tired." She scurried back upstairs.

"Ethan is very upset about Dog," Emma explained.

"So I see," Kurt replied.

"It's funny, really. I never realized he was so attached to him."

"He seems really worried about death," Kurt said.

Emma nodded. "He talks about it every day. I really feel bad for him."

Kurt and Emma stared at each other again.

Well, that exhausts that topic, Emma thought. *God, this is torture.*

"So, are you ready to go?" Kurt asked.

"Yes, just let me get my jacket," Emma

said. She took her short white jean jacket from the front hall closet, then called goodbye up the stairs to Katie and Jane, and she and Kurt walked out the front door.

Kurt turned the music up loud as they drove toward the ocean, which made it easier not to make conversation. When they finally turned onto Shore Boulevard, he lowered the volume. "Want to eat at Aunt Ruby's restaurant?"

Emma hesitated. It was where she and Kurt had gone on their very first date. Emma was sure that Kurt's adopted aunt Ruby, who had embraced Emma as practically one of the family, now hated her like most of Kurt's friends and family. "I don't think so," she finally said.

Kurt shot her a look. "Ruby's not mad at you, if that's what you think."

"That's exactly what I was thinking," Emma admitted.

Kurt gave a short laugh. "Believe it or not, she took me aside before our wedding ceremony and told me that we were too young to get married."

"You never told me that!" Emma exclaimed.

"Well, I never had a reason to tell you," Kurt said. "I thought she was dead wrong . . . at the time."

"I still think I'd rather go somewhere else," Emma said. "Have you been to that new place, Surf's Up?"

"Nope," Kurt said. "That's where they had the fire, right?"

Emma nodded, shuddering at the terrible memory. They had been setting everything up for a party to launch Sunset Magic perfume, and a freak fire had badly damaged the new restaurant and burned Erin Kane's father badly. Erin was a good friend of Emma's and the third backup singer in their rock band, Flirting With Danger. In fact, Mr. Kane was still in rehab.

"So the restaurant is open again?" Kurt asked.

"I heard it was," Emma replied.

They traveled around the bend in the road, and there, jutting out onto the beach, was Surf's Up, clearly back in business. A band was playing on the back deck, where a crowd of people were laughing, eating, and drinking.

Kurt and Emma walked in the front door and were greeted by a blond-haired hostess whose bosom was half spilling out of the top of her tiny hot pink bikini. She wore a hot pink fishnet cover-up over it which Emma noted didn't cover anything up. Kurt and Emma had to make their way through another mass of people, apparently all waiting for tables.

"Hi, welcome to Surf's Up!" the girl called gaily over the loud rock music coming from the deck. "How many are in your party?"

"Two," Kurt replied.

"Nonsmoking or first available?" the girl chirped.

"Nonsmoking," Kurt said firmly.

"Oooo, that means you'll have an hour wait," the blonde said regretfully.

"Coming through, coming through, hot pu-pu platters," a male voice cried.

Kurt stepped back as a tanned, muscular, surfer-jam-clad waiter rushed past with a platter of steaming appetizers balanced on his hand.

"Oh, that dude is so buff!" a girl cried from the bar. "Hey, how much to take him home?"

The hostess placed a lei of plastic flowers labeled seventeen around Kurt's neck. "You can wait in the bar if you want," she suggested. "You'll hear me call your number. And it will also light up over the bar."

Kurt and Emma traded bemused looks, then Kurt took the flowered lei off and handed it back to the hostess. "On second thought," he told her, "never mind." He took Emma's elbow and steered her back out the front door.

When they hit the fresh air, Emma laughed. "They didn't dress like that in there before, I promise you!"

"Now, that's a tourist trap if ever I've wandered into one," Kurt said, making a face. "Remind me to steer clear of that place."

"I don't think I'll have to," Emma said with a laugh.

"Look, how about if we grab some fried clams and just take them out to the beach?" Kurt asked impetuously. "You game?"

"Sure," Emma agreed.

They grabbed an old blanket from Kurt's trunk, and walked down the boardwalk until they found a stand that sold fried clams. Then they stopped into a convenience store for some sodas. They took off their shoes and walked out onto the beach, finally settling down in a deserted spot. For a while they just sat eating and drinking, enjoying the sight of the sun setting over the ocean.

"This is the best," Kurt finally said, dropping the last clam into his mouth. He wiped his hands on a napkin and stuffed the napkin back into the brown paper bag. "Did you get enough to eat?"

Emma nodded and took a sip of her drink. "Clams are just about the only thing I like to eat fried."

"You can't beat Maine fried clams." Kurt leaned back on his elbows and stared out at the darkening ocean. "Look at that," he said quietly. "It's the most beautiful sight in the world."

"No ocean in Michigan," Emma said, trying for a light tone. "Just a lot of lakes."

"And my cousin doesn't even live near any of those," Kurt snorted. He inhaled deeply. "I swear, the air doesn't smell like this anyplace else in the world."

"I know you missed it," Emma said quietly.

Kurt didn't reply.

"I never meant for you to leave, you know," Emma finally said.

Kurt looked over at her. "It wasn't really your decision."

"No, of course not," Emma agreed. She watched the breeze ruffle through his sun-streaked light brown hair, and had to stop herself from leaning over to stroke it back into place. "So . . . you didn't mention how long you were staying."

"No, I didn't," Kurt agreed. He sat up and sifted some sand through his hands. "So, do you want to go get an ice cream or something?"

"Not really," Emma said.

Silence.

"You cold or anything?" Kurt asked.

"No." Emma drew her knees up to her chest and wrapped her arms around them. She took a deep breath. "We might as well admit it. We're so awkward around each other, it hurts."

Kurt gave an uncomfortable laugh. "Yeah, I guess that's true."

"Maybe . . . maybe we're trying too hard," Emma suggested.

"Who knows," Kurt said gruffly. He ran his hand through his hair, a habit Emma remembered him doing whenever he was nervous or anxious.

"Carrie said we should try to be friends again," Emma said.

"Easier said than done," Kurt pointed out. "I mean, how do we go back to that after everything that's happened?"

"I don't know," Emma admitted.

"I'll tell you, it's rough," Kurt said. "My dad is glad to see me, of course, but there's

31

all this pressure from him to never see you again—"

"He hates me—"

"He just doesn't want to see me get hurt again," Kurt said. "You can understand that."

"Well, my parents don't want to see me get hurt again, either," Emma said defensively. "It works both ways, you know."

"I'm not the one who walked out," Kurt said sharply.

"And I'm not the one who pressured and manipulated the other person into getting married—"

"Hey, wait a second," Kurt protested. "I didn't—" He stopped speaking and held up his hand to Emma. "I'm not getting sucked into this." He took a deep breath. "Look, in case you think all I did in Michigan was sit around blaming you, that's not true. You're right, I did pressure you and I did manipulate you. I have to take responsibility for that. I was wrong. And I'm sorry."

Emma felt her heart well up. "Thank you," she whispered.

He ran his hand through his hair again. "Yeah, well, I didn't know I was doing that at the time. Hindsight is twenty-twenty, I guess."

Emma nodded. "I made a lot of mistakes, too. If I could do everything over again, I'd do it so differently. . . ."

"Yeah, like you'd never have said yes when I proposed in the first place."

Emma didn't say a word.

Kurt stared out at the ocean. "I tell myself that if you hadn't said yes, it wouldn't have been a rejection of me, you know? I tell myself that you would have just been rejecting marriage—"

"Which would be exactly right!" Emma broke in. "Because I was too young, I'm still too young—"

"It's more than that," Kurt said.

"And we had problems," Emma admitted reluctantly.

"Big ones," Kurt agreed. "We come from two different worlds, Emma. My family has always had to struggle for money, and you're this rich heiress—"

"I don't think that defines me—"

"Well, in some ways it does," Kurt said. "Okay, so you have a summer job now. But if you lost it tomorrow, it wouldn't change your life at all. You have no idea what it's like to be one paycheck from poverty like most of the people I grew up with—hell, like my own dad. . . ."

"No, I don't," Emma admitted. "But you're the one who made my money into this . . . this defining thing. I don't see it that way."

"I know you don't," Kurt agreed. "Which only points out to me yet again how insulated you are from the real world."

"So what does that mean?" Emma demanded. "I have to stick to my own kind? I had better check out how many millions a guy has before I decide if I like him?"

"Maybe," Kurt said. "Maybe you should."

"You see, it's exactly that kind of stupidity that got in our way!" Emma exclaimed angrily. "I don't care about money! I never have!"

"Emma," Kurt said patiently, "it is only

people who have money who ever have the luxury of making that statement."

Emma thought a moment. "Okay, there's probably some truth to that," she agreed, fiddling with the pearl attached to one of her ears. "But I feel . . . I feel like you blame me for being rich, like it's a bad thing! But money can do a lot of good in this world."

Kurt looked at her. "Do you plan to do good with yours?"

Emma nodded. "I don't inherit most of it until I turn thirty—and then I'll do something really special. I know I will!"

"I believe you," Kurt said. He chuckled. "I wonder where you'll be when you're thirty, Em. I wonder who you'll love."

You! Emma's heart cried, but she bit her lip and remained silent.

Kurt jumped up. "Hey, this conversation is turning entirely too serious. I've got a great idea." He reached for Emma's hand and pulled her up.

"What?"

"Let's go get the hugest ice cream cones

they can build and go play some skee-ball. I'll win you a stuffed animal."

"Okay," Emma agreed, even though it really wasn't what she was in the mood for at all.

They walked toward the boardwalk, the beach blanket rolled up under Kurt's arm. He didn't walk very close to her, or touch her in any way.

This is good, Emma told herself. *We can't go back to being what we were to each other. Not yet.* She looked over at Kurt and a huge lump filled her throat. *Maybe not ever,* she realized. *Maybe no matter what I do or say, or how many different ways we try to hash out our differences, we've lost each other forever.*

THREE

"How many pancakes do you want?" Emma asked Ethan the next morning. She put two on the plate and waited for his answer.

"None," Ethan said, his chin in his hand. "I'm not hungry."

"But you love pancakes," Emma said.

Ethan just shrugged.

Emma sighed. *Ethan is still so upset over Dog,* she realized. *I wish I knew how to help him.*

"I want three pancakes," Katie piped up, holding her new kitten in her arms. "And Snow White wants one, too."

"I hate that stupid cat," Ethan said, narrowing his eyes.

Katie shot Ethan a hurt look and held the kitten closer protectively. It mewed and jumped out of her arms. "Now look what you did!" she cried, and ran after it.

Emma came to sit at the table with Ethan. "I know you feel really bad about Dog," she said gently, "but Katie loves Snow White. Don't take it out on her."

"Yeah," Ethan said grudgingly, staring down at his untied sneakers.

"Your parents made the right decision," Emma said earnestly. "Dog was suffering."

Ethan finally looked up at her. "When my grandfather got sick with cancer a few years ago he suffered, and no one killed him for it!"

Emma thought for a moment. "Sometimes I think we're kinder to animals than we are to people."

"That's not how I see it," Ethan insisted. "I mean, people act like they care about a pet and everything, but it's just . . . just disposable."

Jane and Jeff Hewitt came bounding into the kitchen, laughing, both dressed for tennis. Emma loved her employers, who were very cool people, both lawyers in their thirties. They treated her as if she were a member of the family.

"I'm starved," Jane said. She peered at the stove. "You sweetheart! You made pancakes!" She kissed Emma on the forehead.

"Snow White is under the couch in the living room and she won't come out," Katie reported, coming back into the kitchen. She shot her brother an accusatory look.

There was a knock on the front door.

"I'll get it!" Katie cried, running out of the kitchen.

Emma set two plates of pancakes in front of Jane and Jeff. "Do you want cereal or anything?" she asked Ethan.

He shook his head no. "May I be excused?" he asked his parents.

"No breakfast?" his father asked him, reaching for the maple syrup.

"I'm not hungry," Ethan mumbled.

"So what's up for today?" Jane asked her

son cheerfully. "It's Saturday, so I know you don't have camp." Ethan had a summer job as a counselor-in-training at the new day camp, Club Sunset Island.

Ethan shrugged. "I'm just gonna hang out."

"Eat one pancake, then you can hang out," Jane said.

Emma brought a pancake to Ethan, who looked at it as if it were covered with worms.

"It was the mailman," Katie reported, running back into the room. "We got a postcard from Wills!"

Wills was the other Hewitt child Emma took care of. Currently he was on a week-long camping trip with his Boy Scout troop. Katie handed the postcard to her father.

"Dear Mom, Dad, Ethan, Katie, and Emma," Jeff read out loud. "I'm having fun. I caught some fish but they were little and we threw them back. Stinky got poison ivy because he was stupid and went where the poison ivy was. I didn't get it but I have a lot of mosquito bites. Love, Wills." Jeff laughed and handed the postcard to Jane. "Very eloquent, don't you think?"

"There's a letter for you, Emma," Katie said, handing Emma a beige envelope. "I could read your name on it."

Emma took the letter and inhaled sharply when she saw the return address. It was from Adam Briarly, Sam's half-brother in California, the guy Emma had been having an intense flirtation with for quite some time. Adam was very different from Kurt—artistic, worldly, sophisticated, and very dedicated to becoming a film-maker. For a while Emma had thought that she might even fall in love with Adam, but something kept stopping her. She finally realized that it was because she'd never really stopped loving Kurt.

And then there was that terrible phone call, Emma remembered, *when Adam asked me to finance the screenplay he wrote. I couldn't believe he would do that—use me for my money. On top of everything else, the screenplay was terrible. And when I told him I wouldn't finance it, he hung up on me!*

"If you don't need me right now, I think I'll run up to my room," Emma said.

"Go ahead," Jane agreed. "The kids can clean up from breakfast."

Ethan groaned and Katie began to pout. "I didn't even eat yet!" she exclaimed in a hurt voice.

"You may eat first, you poor, overworked little girl," her mother teased her, pulling her close for a kiss.

"Excuse me," Emma said. She quickly went up to her bedroom, closed the door behind her, then she sat on the bed and tore open Adam's letter.

Dear Emma,

Let's see, what's the stupidest, most immature thing I've done lately? How about hanging up on you? Yep, that must be it. All I can do is apologize and plead temporary insanity. The truth of the matter is I had been up all night doing rewrites on *Frank and Stein,* and I got a little crazy. Well, maybe a lot crazy. You asked me if I was doing speed—I don't even remember what I told you. Well, here's another little truth I'm not so proud of. I was doing more speed than I wanted to admit to anyone, including myself. I guess you could say I got carried away with that intense, artistic thing. Again, that's over, and I apologize for the way I acted.

I don't apologize for asking if you wanted to finance my film, though. I'm sorry you didn't appreciate it, and I guess I'm disappointed, too. Anyway, I did a lot of work on it, and it's just been accepted for a workshop at U.C.L.A. They accept only ten out of about three hundred screenplays that get submitted. I'm hopeful that this is only the beginning.

I'd pick up the phone and call you, but I don't know if you ever want to hear from me again. So I'll just say that I'm thinking about you—daily, hourly, minutely—is that a word?—and I'm hoping that you'll pick up the phone and call me.

Adam

Emma fell back on her bed, the letter still in her hand. *I am shocked,* she thought to herself. *I thought he never wanted to speak to me again.* She sat up and scanned the letter again. When she was about half-way through it, the phone by her bed rang.

"Hewitt residence, Emma speaking," she answered automatically.

"Tell me every single detail about last night," Sam ordered through the phone. "Don't leave out a single thing."

"Hi, Sam," Emma said. "Well, let's see. Kurt has decided to have a sex-change operation and then we're both joining a very spiritual order of nuns together—Our Sisters of Perpetual Confusion."

"You're joking, this is a good sign," Sam said. "Now give me the dirt."

"There isn't any," Emma admitted. "We were ever-so-proper with each other."

"Honest?"

"Honest."

"Well, *quel* drag," Sam commented. "I was hoping to hear you couldn't keep your hands off each other, and he threw you down on the beach, something like that."

"We ate fried clams on the beach, then he told me how much his father hates me, then we started to have a fight, then we didn't have the fight and had ice cream cones instead," Emma reported.

"Excuse me, but is that supposed to make any sense?" Sam asked.

"Sometimes I think my whole life doesn't make much sense," Emma replied, looking at Adam's letter again.

"No good stuff, no clothes torn from each other's bodies, no passionate kisses even?" Sam wondered.

"Zero."

"Wow, serious bummer," Sam said. "Weren't you dying to, like, jump his bones?"

"I don't know," Emma said with a sigh. "I was so happy that he came back to the island—it seemed like a dream. And I've had this fantasy that we'd have another chance . . . but maybe that kind of thing happens only in the movies."

"Well, your life is more like a movie than anyone's I've ever known," Sam pointed out. "If anyone can pull this off, it's you."

"That's just it," Emma replied. "I don't even know what I want. I got a letter from—"

"Sam! Becky's stuck under her bed and I can't pull her out!" Emma heard Allie Jacobs yell.

"Well, push her under it, then!" Sam yelled back.

"I'm serious!" Allie yelled back. "She's stuck and I can't tell if she's laughing or crying!"

Sam groaned into the phone. "Emma? I'll have to call you back after I kill the twins."

"You're not referring to them as 'the monsters,'" Emma noted.

"I must be losing my touch," Sam replied. "Catch you later."

Emma hung up and tucked Adam's letter

into her purse. Just then there was a knock on her door. "Yes?"

The door opened, and Katie stood there with Snow White in her arms. "It's me."

Emma laughed. "I see that."

"I cleaned up the dishes."

"Thank you," Emma replied with a smile.

"Well, Ethan helped, too," Katie admitted. She came over to Emma and sat next to her on the bed. "I have a problem."

"What's that, sweetie?"

"Well, I was thinking maybe you and me could go for a walk on the boardwalk and get some cotton candy," Katie said, stroking Snow White's fur. "Mom said it was okay."

"It sounds like fun," Emma agreed.

"But here's my problem," Katie continued seriously. "I could take Dog for a walk on a leash. But I can't take Snow White for a walk."

"Well, that's one of the differences between having a dog and having a cat for a pet," Emma explained.

Katie nodded. "But Snow White will miss me if I go."

"Oh, I think she'll be okay," Emma assured her.

"I don't know," Katie said. "Mom and Dad are going to play tennis, which means only Ethan will be home, and Ethan hates Snow White."

"He really doesn't hate her, and he'd never hurt her," Emma said. "You know that."

Katie didn't look convinced.

"Come on," Emma said. She got up and slung the shoulder strap of her purse over her shoulder. "We'll go make sure Ethan and Snow White can coexist in peace, and then we'll go check out all the cute guys on the boardwalk."

Katie giggled. "Maybe Kurt will be there!" she cried with excitement. "He's the cutest guy I know!"

As the two of them went downstairs, Emma gave Katie a stern frown. "Now, young lady," she teased, "don't you think he's a little old for you?"

"Oh, no," Katie said breezily. "I like older men!"

*   *   *

"How's the cotton candy?" Emma asked Katie as the two of them strolled hand in hand down the boardwalk.

"Good," Katie said, pulling off a sticky pink gob and stuffing it into her mouth. "I like how it melts on my tongue." She pulled off another piece. "Can I have another one after this?"

Emma reached down and tickled the little girl. "You sound just like Sam!"

Katie giggled and feinted away from Emma. "I don't want to be just like Sam, I want to be just like you!"

"Well, thank you," Emma said. "I'm honored."

"Dang if the two of you aren't the two cutest things on this ol' boardwalk," a male voice with a southern drawl called from behind them.

Emma and Katie turned around, and there was Pres, Sam's boyfriend, standing in front of a kiosk sipping a Coke from a paper cup.

"Hi, there," Emma called happily, leading the little girl over to him. *I really like Pres,* Emma thought. *I always have.*

Press bowed slightly. "Miss Emma, Miss Katie, what are the two of you up to?"

"Emma said we're looking for cute guys," Katie explained.

Emma blushed. "It was a joke," she explained.

Press laughed, and Emma thought again how much she liked him. "So, do I qualify?" he asked Katie.

She thought a moment. "Yeah, I guess so," she decided. "But your hair is too long."

Pres reached back and touched his hair, which was tied back with a leather thong. "You prefer your guys clean-cut?"

Katie nodded seriously. "Like Kurt," she explained.

"Katie's a big Kurt fan," Emma said. "He taught her how to swim. I don't know if you heard, but he's back on the island."

"Sam told me," Pres said. "She said y'all actually ran into him on the beach the day we took Billy to the airport." Pres looked at his watch. "I'm not due back at Wheels for about a half-hour," he said, naming the motorcycle rental store on the boardwalk where he worked part-time. "Can I buy you two a Coke?"

"Hey, Emma, my friend Juliet is over there!" Katie cried, pointing to a black-haired little girl standing in front of a mini amusement park just off the boardwalk. "Juliet!" she yelled. "Juliet!"

The little girl saw Katie and ran over, her mother hurrying after her. Juliet and Katie hugged.

"I missed you!" Juliet said. The little girls hugged again.

"What are you doing?" Katie asked her friend.

"My mom is taking me in to play roller bowling," Juliet said eagerly. "You can win a squirt gun." She turned to her mom. "Can Katie come with us?"

"I'm Juliet's mom, Lorraine Stevens," the woman said, introducing herself. "I've known Katie's parents forever, but we got to the island really late this summer. I don't think we've met."

"I'm Katie's au pair, Emma Cresswell," Emma explained. "And this is my friend, Pres Travis."

"Charmed," she said.

"Can I go with Juliet?" Katie asked Emma.

"I'll be happy to take her," Lorraine said.

"I can come along," Emma offered.

"Oh, it's not necessary, unless you really want to," Lorraine said. "They'll keep each other entertained, and I'll read the book I have stashed away in my purse."

"Are you sure?" Emma said. "I don't want to impose—"

"It's absolutely fine," Lorraine insisted. She took the two little girls by the hand. "I'll have them back here in, say, half an hour. Okay?"

"Fine," Emma agreed, "and thank you."

Lorraine looked back at Emma and grinned. "I was young and single once, too, you know."

Emma sat down at a table with Pres. "She . . . she was just making an assumption that isn't true," she said hastily.

"Uh-huh," Pres said slowly.

"I mean, she thinks we're together or something. I didn't really have time to explain that you're my best friend's boyfriend."

"You cut me to the quick, Emma," Pres said, his hand over his heart. "I thought I was your friend, too."

"Well, you are," Emma said. "Of course you are." *Why am I babbling like an idiot?* Emma asked herself. *Just because you once made the huge error of kissing Pres, and just because you really liked it, and just because you've never told anyone, is no reason to get all flustered with him now!*

Pres leaned over and kissed her cheek. "I'm just funnin' you, Emma. Can I get you a Coke?"

"Sure, thanks," Emma said gratefully.

Pres got her a drink and came back over to the table, setting it in front of her. She took a long sip. "Mmm, thanks."

Pres took a sip of his drink. "I got a letter from Billy today," he told her.

"I got an important letter myself," Emma said before she thought about it.

"Who's yours from?" Pres asked.

"Tell me about Billy first," Emma suggested.

Pres sighed, and stretched his long, cowboy-boot-clad legs out under the table. "There's not much to tell. He's there. I'm here. The Flirts are nowhere."

"But the band means so much to him," Emma protested. "And he loves Carrie so much! He has to come back!"

"Try telling him that," Pres said. "He wants to come back more than anything, but he feels like he has an obligation to stay in Seattle until his dad can run the business again. I guess you could say he's between a rock and a hard place."

Emma hesitated a moment. "Do you think if I sent money—?"

Pres shook his head no and patted Emma's hand. "You know he wouldn't take it. And the issue isn't really money."

Emma groaned. "Why do I have to have friends with so much pride?"

"So, who'd you get a letter from?" Pres asked, crunching some of the ice from his Coke between his teeth.

"Adam," Emma admitted. "Sam's half-brother."

"Oh, yeah," Pres said. "The dude who dragged you out of your wedding."

Emma put her face in her hands. "Don't remind me."

"It was quite a sight," Pres recalled.

"Adam didn't exactly drag me out, you know," Emma said. "I decided I couldn't go through with it."

"Frankly, I felt kind of like dragging you out of there myself," Pres said in a low voice.

Emma looked at him with surprise. "You did? But why?"

"I guess I didn't think you were ready to get married, either."

"But you never said anything," Emma protested.

"Well, it wasn't exactly my place to tell you that, now, was it?" Pres asked.

Emma looked down at the clear nail

polish on her fingernails. "No, I guess not."

"So, what did ol' Adam have to say?" Pres asked, folding his arms over his chest.

"We had a fight over the phone a while ago," Emma explained. "He wanted me to—"

"I heard all about this from Sam," Pres interrupted. "You know that girl is a walking gossip column."

"Well, in the letter he apologized," Emma said, "and he said that he thinks about me every day, and he wants me to call him."

"I can't say that I blame him," Pres said with a lazy grin. "And you and Kurt are—?"

"I don't know," Emma admitted. "I went out with him last night. I just feel so confused—"

Pres reached over again and took Emma's hand. "It's okay to be confused, Emma. You don't have to have the whole world figured out."

"Gee, look who's here!" a voice cried, a little too loud and a little too gay.

Emma turned. It was Sam, striding over

to their table. Sam's eyes locked on Pres's hand on Emma's, and a brittle grin swept over her face. "While the cat's away the micey will play, huh, you furry little rodents?"

"We just ran into each other," Emma explained. She could feel the heat coming to her cheeks. *I have no reason to feel guilty,* she told herself. She took back her hand.

"Oh, I'm just teasing you two," Sam said, sitting down next to Pres. "I just stopped into Wheels and they told me you were on your lunch break, so I came to look for you."

"I'm glad you did," Pres told her, kissing her lightly. "You look pretty."

"Don't try to distract me from catching the two of you together," Sam said sternly.

"I was taking a walk with Katie and we ran into Pres—"

Sam looked around. "Well, you're in big trouble, Em, because you've lost the kid now."

"She went with a friend to play some games in the arcade," Emma explained.

"Oh, sure," Sam said.

"She did!" Emma insisted.

"Emma, I'm teasing you," Sam said, "So, listen, how about we all go hang at the Play Café tonight? Some new band is supposed to be playing. I want to see if they're any good."

"It'll just be depressing, seein' as we've had to cancel all our gigs until Billy gets back," Pres said.

"Hey, we have to keep an eye on the comp," Sam insisted. "Besides, I just have a feeling Billy is going to come back really soon."

"I hope you're right," Pres said. "Because I'm startin' to get real depressed about this whole thing."

"So write some sad songs," Sam suggested, linking her arm with his. She leaned over and nuzzled Pres's neck. "Or better yet, use me for inspiration." She began to kiss Pres.

Well, I certainly feel dumb sitting here while they kiss, Emma thought. Pres delicately pulled away from Sam just as Emma stood up. "I'd better go find Katie," she said.

"Try to meet us tonight," Sam urged, her arms around Pres's neck.

"I will," Emma promised.

As Emma walked toward the arcade, she could feel Sam's eyes on her back, watching her.

Pres is my friend and he's Sam's boy-friend, Emma said to herself. *I would never, ever do anything to hurt my friendship with Sam.*

I only hope that Sam knows that.

FOUR

"So, is Kurt coming over?" Sam asked Emma, yelling over the music blaring out of the jukebox.

It was that evening, and Emma was at the Play Café with Sam, Carrie, Erin, Pres, and two other members of the Flirts, Jay Bailey, who played keyboards, and Jake Fisher, their new drummer. Jake had replaced their long-time drummer, Sly Smith, who was very ill with the AIDS virus.

"I didn't invite him," Emma admitted, pushing some blond hair behind one ear.

"Why not?" Sam asked.

Emma shrugged. *Because I don't even*

know how to act with him in private yet, she wanted to say, *having him here with all of you watching us would be excruciating.*

"I'm serious, Em," Sam said. "I can't believe you didn't ask him!"

"Don't pressure Emma," Pres said. "Between that letter she got from Adam and all this stuff with Kurt, she needs a little time to sort everything out."

Sam cocked her head at Emma. "What letter?"

"I got a letter from Adam today," Emma explained.

"Uh-huh," Sam said. "So how come Pres knew about it and I didn't?"

"I started to tell you on the phone, but Becky was stuck under a bed or something, if you recall," Emma reminded her.

Sam's eyes narrowed. "I don't remember you starting to tell me about a letter from Adam." She turned to Carrie. "Did you know about it?"

"No," Carrie said. "Don't make such a big deal out of it."

"I'm not," Sam said, tightening the ponytail holder around her hair. "I'm just a little surprised Pres knew about it before we did."

This conversation can lead nowhere good, Emma thought, so she quickly changed the subject. "So, who's this band that's playing here tonight?"

"They're called Live Wire," Jake reported. He and Erin were dating pretty seriously, and he was sitting with his arm draped around her shoulders. "Two girls and two guys from Portland—I heard through the grapevine that they're really good."

"We'll be the judge of that," Sam said officiously. She craned her neck around, looking for the waitress. "Didn't we order that pizza about an hour ago?"

"Ten minutes, hungry lady," Pres said, giving her shoulder a squeeze. He looked her over. "Hey, is that a Samstyles you have on?" he asked her.

Samstyles was the clothing line that Sam designed for the Cheap Boutique.

Since she couldn't sew, all her original designs were held together with pins.

"Yeah," Sam said preening. "What do you think?" She was wearing a white cotton antique lace slip partly covered by sheer white material wound around and around her like a mummy's wrappings. A row of scattered tiny red heart-shaped rhinestone pins held it all together. And of course on her feet were her trademark red cowboy boots.

"I think you are an original, girl," Pres told her.

"Is that original good or original bad?" Sam asked.

"Definitely good," Pres assured her. He sniffed her neck. "You smell good, too."

"Ah, the wonderful aroma of Sunset Magic," Sam intoned. "Does it make me irresistible?" She wiggled her eyebrows at him comically.

"Hey, I know that girl!" Erin said, pointing to a tiny girl in denim hot pants who was talking to one of the roadies on the stage. "Her name is Penny . . . something-

or-other. She was in my music comp class at Emerson last year. Hey, Live Wire must be her band! She's great!"

"And cute," Jay added.

"And about a size three," Erin pointed out. "Maybe I should just kill her."

Emma smiled at Erin. With her long, wild blond hair and beautiful high-cheekboned face, Erin was really attractive. But she was also significantly overweight—maybe fifty pounds or so. *It certainly doesn't stop her from being great looking,* Emma thought, admiring Erin's outfit of a beige lace baby-doll top over black jeans and hiking boots.

"Try to control yourself," Jake said, reaching for his beer, "the Flirts need you."

"If there still *is* a Flirts," Jay said glumly.

"Of course there's a Flirts," Emma said. "Right, Carrie?"

"What?" Carrie said, sounding dazed. Emma could see that she'd been lost in thought. The record ended but the loud voices all around them still made it difficult to hear.

"I said there's still a Flirts," Emma repeated. "Billy is coming back. Soon. Right?"

Carrie sighed heavily. "Don't ask me, because I don't know." She fiddled with the straw in her Diet Coke. "Maybe if I just went to visit him in Seattle . . . if I could just be there with him for a couple of days . . ."

"What good would that do?" Jay asked. "Unless you could talk him into coming back, that is."

"Maybe I should go with you and try to talk sense into that boy," Pres drawled. "We've already canceled three gigs. If we have to cancel any more, we might as well hang the whole thing up—our rep will be totally shot."

The roadies were setting up various amps and equipment onstage. *It should be us about to go on,* Emma thought.

"Maybe . . . maybe we should replace Billy," Jay said in a low voice.

Pres's face turned dark. "Don't ever say that, man."

"But what if Billy doesn't come back?" Jay asked.

"He's coming back," Pres insisted through thin lips.

"Heads up, heads up, coming through with the pizza," the waitress Marie yelled, rushing over to their table with the huge pie. "Here you go," she said, passing out plates. "Anybody need anything else?"

"An order of nachos with everything, please," Sam said, reaching for a slice of pizza.

"Coming up," she said on the run.

"Where do you put it?" Erin asked in awe.

Sam shrugged. "I eat more when I get upset," she said, "and talking about Billy really tweaks me."

Carrie heaved another huge sigh.

"We've got to cheer up!" Sam cried. "He's not dead! It's Sly who has AIDS, not Billy. It's Sly we should be worried about!"

"There's not much we can do for him other than write him and call him," Emma pointed out, "and we do that all the time."

"I feel like the whole world is falling apart," Jay said gloomily. He looked at the pizza and made a face. "I definitely can't eat now."

"Okay, all you partiers, listen up!" the emcee yelled into the microphone. "I heard this band in Portland, and I gotta tell you, I was blown away. So put your hands together for Live Wire!"

Everyone at their table offered their restrained applause. The girl Erin knew and another girl with long, straight brown hair ran onstage, along with a cute, short guy with a buzz cut and a long-haired guy in sunglasses.

"Sunglasses in a club, *très* pretentious," Sam opined, biting into her pizza.

"One, two, one-two-three-four," the short guy called into the microphone, and the band went into their first number. It was much more heavy metal than the Flirts, a real wall of sound. Emma could barely make out the lyrics they were singing, something about going crazy followed by a lot of screaming. When they finished their first song the applause was enthusiastic but not overwhelming.

"Big deal," Sam scoffed. "They sound like they're all being electrocuted, if you ask me."

"Maybe that's how they got their name," Carrie said.

Live Wire played for forty minutes, then they took a break.

"So, what do we think?" Jake asked the group.

"They suck," Sam decreed.

"Penny—that keyboard player—is really good," Jay admitted.

"You're better," Erin told him loyally.

Sam nudged Emma in the ribs hard. "Hey, isn't that Sheldon Plotkin from Polimar Records over there?" she hissed, pointing to a table on the other side of the room.

"I think it is," Emma agreed. She looked over at Pres with trepidation. Polimar was the label that was interested in the Flirts. "Do you think he's scouting Live Wire?" she asked Pres.

"I don't know, but I'm gonna go find out,"

Pres said in a steely voice. "Excuse me." He got up and ambled across the room.

"Well, if I was a drinking kind of guy, I'd say this would be a good time to get drunk," Jay said.

They all watched Pres talking with Sheldon Call-me-Shelly Plotkin, then they watched him cross back over to them.

"He's scouting them, all right," Pres informed them as he settled back into his seat next to Sam. "He told me he thinks they're really good. And then he wanted to know when he can hear the Flirts again."

"What did you say?" Carrie asked.

"I said probably within the next couple of weeks," Pres told her. "I told him we were working up some new tunes."

"Why didn't you just tell him the truth?" Emma wondered.

"Emma, that dude has zero interest in the personal problems of Billy, or any of us for that matter. I wasn't about to give him a reason to blow us off."

"So what happens if Billy isn't back in a couple of weeks?" Jay asked anxiously.

"That's a real good question," Pres said, reaching for his glass of iced tea. "Unfortunately, I don't have a real good answer."

When Carrie dropped Emma off at the Hewitts' it was after midnight, and she tiptoed into the house to make sure she didn't wake anybody. Her mind was on a million things, none of them good—Kurt, Adam, Billy, Sly, the band—and so she was completely startled when she heard the voice.

"Hi." It came from the darkened family room off the front hall, and Emma just about jumped out of her skin.

"Ethan?" Emma whispered. "Is that you?"

"Yeah, it's me."

"What are you doing up so late sitting here in the dark?" Emma asked him. She went to turn on the light.

"No, don't," he told her quickly.

She went to sit next to him on the couch. "Are you okay?"

"I couldn't sleep," he told her.

"Do you want to talk?" Emma asked. As her eyes got used to the dark she could make out his profile and the dejected slump of his shoulders.

"You don't have to," Ethan said.

"It's okay, really," Emma assured him. "Is it about Dog?"

Ethan nodded. "I know it's dumb, but I keep thinking about him."

"It's not dumb," Emma said quietly.

"I keep thinking how he must have felt—like we all deserted him! He must have been so scared, don't you think?"

"I don't know," Emma said honestly. "But I don't think it would have been any easier for Dog or for you if he were still alive and in pain, getting sicker and sicker every day."

"Well, maybe he would have gotten better," Ethan said.

"No, Ethan—"

"How do you know?" Ethan asked, "you don't! Some people with cancer get better! We never gave Dog a chance!"

"Ethan—"

"And I don't believe he's in some stupid doggie heaven, either," Ethan continued. "He's just gone, just dead, the end."

"Everything that's alive has to die sometime," Emma said gently.

"Well, I hate it," Ethan said viciously, and Emma could hear the tears in his voice that he was trying to hold back. "It really, really sucks."

Emma put her arm around Ethan's shoulder, and she felt the tears wracking his body. She just sat there with him, not saying a word. When she felt his shudders lessen, she leaned forward and handed him a tissue from the box on the table. He blew his nose loudly a couple of times.

"I was thinking," Emma said. "Tomorrow Kurt and I are going snorkeling. Why don't you come along, and invite Dixie." Emma was referring to thirteen-year-old Dixie Mason, Ethan's very first girlfriend. Dixie was visiting her cousin Molly Mason for the summer, and she, too, was a counselor-in-training at Club Sunset Island.

"Tomorrow's Sunday," Ethan said, his

voice sounding nasal from crying. "It's your day off. You don't want me and Dixie tagging along."

"I wouldn't have invited you if I didn't want you along," Emma said. "And I like Dixie. Besides, you'd be doing me a favor. Things are kind of up in the air between Kurt and me—it'll make it easier to have another couple along."

Even in the dark Emma could see Ethan sit up straighter on the couch. "If you're sure . . ."

"I'm sure," Emma said firmly, getting up from the couch. "I'll call Kurt in the morning, and you can call Dixie, okay?"

"Okay," Ethan said.

"Well, good night, then," Emma called from the doorway.

"Emma?"

"Yes?"

"Thanks," Ethan said. "For . . . you know. It kinda helped, just talking about it."

Emma smiled toward the sensitive young boy across the room. *It's amazing how helping someone else with his problems helps you forget about your own,* she thought to herself. "Ethan," she said warmly, "that's what friends are for."

FIVE

"There's nothing too tough about snorkeling," Kurt told Emma, Ethan, and Dixie the next morning. "There's just a few simple rules for using the mask—"

"Uh, Kurt?" Ethan interrupted. "I already know how to snorkel. You taught me last summer at the country club, remember?"

"Oh, right," Kurt agreed with a sheepish smile. He turned to Emma. "I suppose you're covered on all of this, too."

"I am," Emma agreed, fixing the narrow strap of her pink and white striped tank suit.

"Well, I'm not, y'all!" Dixie exclaimed.

"Starkville, Mississippi, is pretty well land-locked, and this summer is my very first trip to an ocean!"

It was about ten A.M. and the four of them had traveled to a deserted part of the beach far off the beaten path. There was a water reservoir created by large rock formations where Kurt had told them they could easily snorkel in the calm water.

When Emma had called him and asked if Ethan and Dixie could come along, he had readily agreed. Emma had told him that Ethan was upset about Dog, and besides, she knew Kurt liked being a role model for younger kids.

"Ethan, why don't you show Dixie?" Kurt suggested. "I have something I need to discuss with Emma." Kurt led Emma a little way down the beach.

"Yes?" Emma asked.

"Nothing," Kurt said. "I just thought it would be good to let Ethan be the one to show her."

Emma smiled at him. *That is just so Kurt,* she thought to herself. *He's so sensi-*

tive to kids. She looked over at the two younger teens. Dixie was listening avidly to everything Ethan was telling her. *She looks so cute in her red bikini,* Emma thought. *She's so tiny and blond and Ethan is so dark, they really do make a darling couple.*

"Are you thinking about how cute they look?" Kurt asked her.

Emma laughed. "How did you know?"

"I know that look you get on your face," Kurt explained. He looked over at Dixie. "You know, she could be your sister."

"You think?" Emma asked.

Kurt nodded. "She really does look kind of like you." He looked back at Emma. "Were you that cute when you were thirteen?"

"I doubt it," Emma admitted. "I was totally under my mother's fashion thumb. I wore little designer dresses and had my hair perfectly coiffed at my mother's hairdresser in Paris."

"Well, let's see," Kurt said, folding his arms, "when I was thirteen I had a paper route so I could afford to buy the jeans I really wanted, and my mom gave me all my haircuts."

"I have a feeling you had more fun than I did," Emma said softly.

Kurt looked thoughtful. "Maybe I did at that." His eyes scanned her body. "Hey, did you put on enough sunblock?"

"I couldn't reach my back," Emma admitted.

"So, what were you going to do, just not protect half of your skin?" Kurt asked.

"I could ask Dixie . . ."

"Emma," Kurt said in a low voice, "do you really not want me touch you that badly?"

"No," Emma replied, feeling flustered. "You can do it. I mean, it's fine if you do it. . . ."

Kurt reached into the canvas beach bag and brought out the sunscreen. "Turn around," he told her.

Emma turned her back to him. She felt the sunscreen squirt on to her back, and then she felt Kurt's strong, sure hand rubbing the cream into her skin. At first it felt very businesslike, but then, as the cream began to sink into her skin, Kurt's touch grew more languorous. He made firm, lazy circles on her back, stroking the muscles until she closed her eyes and practically purred with pleasure.

"Feel good?" Kurt asked her, leaning close to her ear.

"Mmmmm," Emma breathed. "It's heavenly."

His fingers began kneading the tense muscles in the back of her neck, and slowly she felt the tension ooze away, until she was half leaning into Kurt's arms.

"Well, we're ready!" Ethan said, running over to them.

Kurt moved a step away from Emma. "Oh, cool," Kurt said. "You guys have sunscreen on, right?"

"The waterproof kind," Dixie said.

"Okay, let's go meet some fish," Kurt said. "Your swim fins are over there," he added, nodding to a pile of fins near the mouth of the water reservoir. When Ethan and Dixie had walked away, he turned back to Emma. "I can finish that later, if you want."

"I . . . don't think I'll need anymore sun-block," Emma said.

"That's not what I meant," Kurt replied. "That's not what I meant at all."

That night around sunset Emma walked along the beach, lost in thought. The beach was practically empty now, with the only the rare couple or family still sitting on a blanket, loathe to let go of the day. Farther down the beach a crowd was playing rap music so loud that the beat carried all the way to where Emma was.

She sighed and pulled her jean jacket a little more tightly around her. *I had a great time snorkeling with Kurt this morning,* she thought. *But then he made some excuse about something he had to do with his family tonight, and he just dropped me off with Ethan and Dixie.* She sighed and idly reached for a seashell, and threw it out at the ocean. *Maybe it's just as well,* she thought. *We really need to talk more before we—*

"We can't go on meeting like this," a husky southern-accented voice said from behind her.

Emma turned around. "Pres!" she said with surprise. "What are you doing here?"

He laughed. "Probably the same thing you're doing here."

"Of course," Emma replied. *Now, why did I say something that stupid?* she asked herself. *Running into him twice unexpectedly in two days isn't so unusual, is it?*

"I came out to meditate on the sunset," he told her, his hands deep in the pockets of his worn jeans. "Looks like you had the same notion."

Emma looked out at the ocean. "I love the beach this time of day," she said softly.

"Me, too. Sometimes when I get stuck writing a tune and I feel like I'm about to explode, I just come out here and look out at the ocean under that big ol' setting sun, and I realize my writing problems are real small potatoes."

Emma smiled at him, and he scrutinized her face. "You're lookin' a little crispy around the edges, girl."

Emma touched her face, which was warm from spending the day in the sun. "I was out snorkeling with Kurt," she explained. "I used a sunblock, but I have a feeling I didn't reapply it often enough."

"Does it hurt?"

"Not really," Emma replied, "but I'll probably peel."

They were quiet for a moment, both enjoying the beauty of the setting sun.

"So, you went out with Kurt, huh?" Pres asked.

Emma nodded. "It was fun."

"That's good," Pres said.

"But we didn't talk," Emma continued. "Not about anything important, I mean."

"Well, I thought that's how you wanted it for now," Pres said.

Emma sighed and kicked her bare foot into the sand. "I don't know what I want."

Pres chuckled. "Now you sound like Sam."

"Sam knows what she wants," Emma said. "She wants you."

"At the moment," Pres said lightly, scratching at the day's growth of beard on his chin. "Hey, did you call Sam's brother in California?"

"No," Emma admitted.

"Do you want to?"

"I don't know!" She laughed self-consciously. "I feel so . . . so up in the air about everything!"

"Including the band, I reckon," Pres said.

"Yeah, there's that, too," Emma agreed. She took in the forlorn look on Pres's face. "I know it's much harder for you than it is for me. For any of us, probably—except Carrie."

"Sometimes I think it would be easier if I just knew . . . something," Pres said in a ragged voice. "Something, one way or the other." He knelt down and picked up a handful of sand, then let it fall slowly through his fingers. "Right now everything feels like this sand," he said, "just slipping away, nothing to show for it, all that work, all for nothing. . . ."

Emma knelt quickly beside him. "Don't say that! It isn't true!"

"That's how it feels—"

"You and Billy have worked so hard. It can't be over—"

"Yeah," Pres said softly, but he sounded dubious.

"You just can't give up," Emma said. "It's like Sam with her birth parents—"

"No, it ain't nothing like that," Pres interrupted. "Look how lucky she got! She found her birth mother right away. And then her father—well, that was nothing short of a miracle. Do you know how long I've been searching for my birth mother? Or how many years Billy and I have put into the Flirts?"

Emma reached out and touched Pres's arm. "You're right. That was dumb of me. There really isn't any comparison—"

"Why, Lorell, do you see what I see?" an all-too-familiar voice taunted from behind them. Emma turned around to face Diana

De Witt and Lorell Courtland, the two most hateful girls on Sunset Island. Both were impeccably dressed, Diana in white jeans and a tiny white lace T-shirt that bared her tanned stomach, and Lorell in a sheer flower-print minidress with matching hair ribbon.

"Well, I have to say I am just shocked," Lorell trilled. "Imagine finding Emma Cresswell and Pres Travis practically *doin' it* right here on the beach!"

Emma and Pres stood up and faced the girls. "Go away," Emma said in her frostiest voice. "We are having a private conversation."

"It looks like you're having a lot more than a conversation," Diana said, an eyebrow raised.

"You're right," Pres said solemnly. "You caught us. I was just about to throw Emma down in the sand and ravish her. You stopped me just in time."

"We wouldn't dream of cutting into your fun," Lorell said innocently. "But I have to say I'm just shocked that you'd sneak off behind Sam's back this way!"

"We aren't sneaking behind anyone's back—" Emma protested.

"No?" Diana asked. She ostentatiously looked off to the right and then to the left. "But I don't see Sam anywhere. And as we all know, anyone as tall and gawky as her is hard to miss!"

"Yep, dang if you haven't caught us," Pres said. "Oh, the shame of it."

Diana raised one elegant eyebrow again. "I wouldn't be joking about something like this if I were you."

"But, Diana honey," Lorell exclaimed, "if you were Pres, you'd be dating Samantha Bridges, and that would be just the lowest, wouldn't it?"

"Actually," Diana said, pushing some windblown hair off her face, "I think sneaking around behind her back is even lower."

Emma gave a harsh laugh. "Diana, really, you are the last person on this island who should be giving anyone a lecture on morals or ethics."

Diana tossed her hair back. "See, the difference between you and me, Emma, is that I've always been honest about who I am. On the other hand, underneath your oh-so-sweet, pious exterior, you are sneaky and underhanded. And one of these days everyone on this island is going to know the truth."

"Look, Diana—" Emma began to say.

"Oh, that's right," Diana recalled, "most people already found out how low you are when you walked out on the guy you loved and humiliated him in front of everyone—"

"Such a shame," Lorell added piously.

"And now you're trying to steal your best friend's guy," Diana admonished Emma.

"I know this might be hard for your little ol' brain to comprehend, Diana," Pres said, "but Emma and I are friends."

"I'll bet," Diana said sarcastically. She turned to Lorell. "Let's go. The air here is getting a little thick."

"Bye-bye, lovebirds!" Lorell called out as she and Diana continued down the beach.

When they were gone, Emma gave a

self-conscious laugh. "Gee, I really thought I was going to be alone out here so I could do some thinking."

"Are you sorry I ran into you?" Pres asked.

"No, not at all," Emma replied. "I find it so easy to talk to you. I always have."

"I feel that way about you, too," Pres said in a low voice.

Suddenly an image of being in Pres's arms filled Emma's head. *I remember exactly how it felt to kiss him,* she recalled, the heat coming to her sunburned face. *I remember how much my body wanted him to keep kissing me and how awful and guilty I felt. It lasted only a moment but—*

"You know, I've never understood those two," Pres said, breaking into Emma's thoughts. "I used to just think they were harmless, kind of funny even, but I'm beginning to wonder about that."

"I've *always* wondered about that," Emma said, trying to sound lighthearted. "Imagine them trying to make something out of our running into each other on the beach. I mean, it's totally innocent. And we're friends. Good friends. We can have a conversation on the beach if we want to. It's so silly, really!"

Pres stared at her. "Yeah, silly."

"Because we're just friends," Emma said again, staring back at Pres.

"Right," Pres agreed, his voice low and intimate.

She was standing not more than two inches from him. She could feel the heat of him, and her heart was beating faster in her chest. She could count each breath that raised his chest.

"Hey, how about we go to the Play Café and play some pool?" Pres finally asked, taking a step away from her.

The moment was broken. Emma was glad. Because that moment had felt all too dangerous for her to deal with.

SIX

"Sam wasn't home," Pres reported as he made his way back to the table at the Play Café, where he'd left Emma. "I got a recording made by one of the twins, who said that if I was Ian calling, I had better have a good excuse for not showing up at the movie."

"It must have been Becky," Emma said. "She and Ian are having problems with their relationship."

Pres settled into the booth across from Emma. "Somehow relationship problems when you're fourteen don't seem as tough as they do at twenty-one."

"But you and Sam don't have any relationship problems," Emma pointed out.

"Not now," Pres agreed. "We sure did, though." A boisterous group standing near the jukebox all laughed at once, and someone turned up the volume on the TV monitor, which was tuned into MTV. "You want me to go sign up for the pool table?"

"Not really," Emma admitted. "I'm not very good."

"What we need is Carrie," Pres said. "That girl is a ringer on the pool table."

"Her brothers taught her." Emma folded her hands primly on the table. "So . . ." The rest of the sentence never followed. *Why do I feel so self-conscious?* Emma thought. *This is just ridiculous!*

"So," Pres echoed, a teasing lilt to his voice. "Emma, relax. We tried calling Sam to ask her to join us, and she isn't home. We're allowed to hang out together, you know."

"I know that," Emma said. "Of course I know that."

"Well, good," Pres said. "Now, let's see if we can rustle up the waitress." He looked around the room to no avail. "It's a zoo in here."

"Every night is," Emma pointed out. "We're just used to it."

Pres fiddled with the earring in his left earlobe. "So, do you want to call Kurt and see if he wants to come on over here?"

Emma sighed. "He made it pretty clear he didn't want to be with me tonight," she admitted.

"Listen, I know this is none of my business," Pres began, "but . . . no, forget it."

"What?" Emma asked.

"I've been hanging with Sam too long," Pres said. "I was just about to get into your business, which is somewhere that I do not belong."

"I really want to hear what you were going to say," Emma insisted.

Pres hesitated. "Okay," he finally said, "though I may end up regretting this. You act like it's you who did Kurt wrong, like it's you who has to make something up with him. But he's the one who couldn't love you for who you are, and in my experience that never, ever works."

"People change," Emma said in a low voice.

Pres nodded. "I reckon they do sometimes. And I like Kurt. He's a good guy. But if you want to get together with him again, he's the one who needs to do the changing."

"I hurt him—"

"Well, dang, girl, he hurt you, too!" Pres exclaimed. "Okay, what you did was more visible to the world, maybe, but what he did to you was even worse. He fell in love with a girl, and then he tried to make that girl into someone else. . . ."

Emma smiled. "How did you get so smart?"

"By making a whole hell of a lot of mistakes," Pres said with a grin. "Hey, I was thinking—"

"This is so touching!" Diana cried, sashaying over to their table, drink in hand. "First the two of you get down and dirty—or should I say sandy—on the beach, and now you come in here for a little post-sex bite to eat!" She leaned over their table confidentially. "I understand completely. Great sex always makes me hungry, too." Her eyes roamed over Pres. "Although you and I would have to get up close and personal before I could tell for sure . . . about the 'great' part, I mean."

"Diana, you may find this hard to believe," Pres said with amusement, "but I have no desire in this world to get up close and personal with you."

"Oh, I could change your mind," she assured him, running her fingers down her tanned neck. "It's a shame about Billy having to leave the island, by the way."

"Thank you for those words of concern," Emma said coldly. "Now go far away."

"In a moment," Diana said, her eyes still on Pres. "I just thought I'd let you know that I'm available to sing lead in Billy's place."

"Please—" Emma snorted.

"Uh, uh, uh, don't answer too quickly!" Diana insisted. "Right now you have no band at all. I happen to be rich enough to make the band happen big-time. And I'm talented enough to back that up."

"Well, it's good to know that you don't lack for confidence," Pres told her.

"Diana, you seem to forget that you were kicked out of the Flirts," Emma said.

"Oh, I haven't forgotten," Diana said, sipping her drink. "You hired that lard-ass girl—what's her name—Erwin?"

"Erin," Emma corrected her.

"Whatever," Diana said breezily. "Anyway, everyone knows the band went totally downhill after I left." She turned back to Pres. "By the way, now that I see you and Sam are finished, why don't you give me a call sometime. About the band . . . or just any little thing." She winked at Pres and sauntered off.

"Why didn't you tell her you and Sam are still together?" Emma asked.

"Why should I bother?" Pres asked. "It's not like I give two hoots for what she thinks."

"That's true," Emma said with a sigh. "I

wish I could be more like you. I always seem to—"

"Well, well, this is definitely one for the *Breakers* gossip column," Kristy Powell said, stopping by their table with a cute guy Emma had never seen before.

Kristy was a rich girl who wrote for the island's newspaper. She was a major flirt who—to everyone's surprise—had shown up on the island that summer engaged. But this guy was definitely not the same guy she'd been calling her fiancé.

"Hello, Kristy," Emma said. "And sorry, this is not one for your gossip column."

"No?" Kristy asked. "Resident Heiress Emma Cresswell and southern rock stud-muffin Pres Travis were seen recently gazing lovingly into each other's eyes at the Play Café," Kristy recited as if she were reading her column out loud. "Neither Emma's on-again/off-again boyfriend, Kurt Ackerman, newly returned to the island after a major scandal, or Sam Bridges, Pres's supposed squeeze, were anywhere in sight. When asked to comment on this, the hot couple said—?"

"We aren't a couple," Emma insisted.

"The hot couple said we aren't a couple," Kristy finished, making it clear from her tone of voice that she didn't believe Emma for a second. She turned to her companion. "This is my friend Greg Long, by the way."

"What happened to the fiancé?" Pres asked.

Kristy linked arms with Greg. "Greg happened, I guess," she replied. "Well, thanks for the hot gossip, you young lovers. See ya!"

"I can't take any more of this," Emma said with disgust. "Let's just get out of here."

"You got it," Pres agreed.

They made their way through the crowd and were just about to open the door of the cafe, when it was pushed open. By Sam.

"Hi!" Emma cried.

"Hi," Sam said in a flat voice. She looked from Emma to Pres and back at Emma. "What's going on?"

"Nothing!" Emma said quickly.

Sam looked at Pres. "I thought you were writing music tonight."

"I was," Pres said. "But I got stuck and went for a walk on the beach, and I ran into Emma." He leaned forward to give Sam a kiss on the lips, but she turned her head so that he hit her cheek.

"It's kind of funny, isn't it?" Sam asked. "I mean, you guys just happened to run into each other yesterday."

"It's just a coincidence," Emma assured her. "We tried to call you, actually, just a few minutes ago, to see if you could come join us!"

Sam pushed some red curls behind one ear. "I dropped the twins at the movies. I have to go pick them up later. . . ." Her voice trailed off. "Did you guys really try to call me?"

"We sure did, sweet thing," Pres assured her.

"So, then, there's a message on the answering machine at the Jacobs' house from you, right?" Sam asked.

"Well, no," Pres said. "I didn't leave a message."

Sam gave Pres a cold look. "You didn't, huh? How convenient."

"He's telling you the truth," Emma insisted. "Sam, please, I would never do anything to hurt you—"

"Hey, darlin', think about it," Pres said. "If I was gonna carry on some secret thing with Emma, I wouldn't pick the most public place on the island, now, would I? Everyone knows this club is gossip central."

"That's true," Sam said, relenting a little. She moved closer to Pres, and he put his arm around her. "So, how was your date with Kurt?" she asked Emma.

"It was really nice," Emma replied, "but then he ended it early . . . and I don't really know why."

"Bummer," Sam commented tersely.

"How's Bubba?" Emma asked, trying to fill in the strained silence.

"The greatest," Sam said. "The twins love him, and Dan Jacobs is so in lust with this Kiki Coors babe he's dating, he doesn't seem to know what's going on in the house, anyway."

"Good," Emma replied. "I mean, good that everything is okay with Bubba, not good that Dan doesn't know what's going on in his own house."

"I knew what you meant," Sam said stiffly.

"So, where's your usual great advice for me about Kurt?" Emma asked lightly.

"Maybe you should just go over to his house and tear his clothes off."

"Well, that's one solution I hadn't considered," Emma said. She smiled at Sam, and Sam smiled back, but Emma could tell that Sam wasn't completely convinced that nothing was going on behind her back. "Look, I really should go," Emma said. "Now that the two of you have found each other—"

"You don't have to do that," Sam said quickly.

"No, really, I—"

"Emma, don't get weird on me," Sam said. "What are you gonna do if you leave?"

"Oh, go read a book or something," Emma said.

"Now, that is mondo boring," Sam decreed. "I will share my studly guy with you for the evening, because that's just the kind of confident babe I am."

Pres kissed Sam, and this time his kiss landed on her lips. "Hey, did I mention what a cool lady you are?" he asked her.

"Why, no," Sam said, eagerly awaiting his compliment.

"Just checking," Pres teased.

Sam bumped him with her hip. "As you can see, Emma, I chose beauty over brains. Hey, maybe we should call Kurt, what do you guys think?"

Emma heaved a sigh of relief. *Sam finally sounds normal,* she thought to herself. "Let's leave it be for now," Emma said. "I'm not going to throw myself at him."

"Okay," Sam agreed. "So how about if we call Carrie? Oh, no, wait, she told me she's working . . ."

Someone turned the speakers up even

louder and the sound of Metallica crashed through the air.

"So, where were you guys headed?" Sam yelled over the music.

"Someplace to eat," Pres said. "It's so crowded in here tonight, we couldn't even find a waitress." He pulled Sam close. "I know you're always hungry, so you pick the spot."

"Mmm, let's see, what am I in the mood for?" Sam mused. "How about Mexican food? There's a new place over by—"

"Sam, you're looking almost normal tonight!" Diana crowed, coming their way again. "I mean jeans and a cropped denim vest—you look kind of cute!"

Sam laughed. "Hey, Diana, did you just kind-of, sort-of give me a compliment?"

"Yeah," Diana replied, "I did."

"Thanks," Sam said with a grin. "I'll take all the compliments I can get, even from you!"

"I've got to hand it to you, Sam," Diana said, "you are really taking this well."

"What? Your giving me a compliment?"

Sam asked. "I mean, I know it's a rare thing, but—"

"That's not what I meant," Diana interrupted. "I meant the fact that you just caught your best friend with your boyfriend."

"Give it a rest, Diana," Emma snapped.

"Look, Sam has a right to know," Diana insisted. "I caught them on the beach together, Sam—"

"Diana, no one wants to hear—" Pres began.

"I want to hear," Sam said.

"Come on!" Emma exclaimed. "This is Diana De Witt! You don't want to hear her lies!"

"Maybe I do," Sam said in a level voice. She folded her arms. "Talk."

"Well, Lorell and I were taking a walk around sunset," Diana said. "We were way down the beach, past the Long Wharf. You know, where couples always go to do it . . ."

"This is disgusting—" Emma began, but the fire in Sam's eyes shut her up.

"Anyway, we stumbled over Emma and Pres there in the sand, and they were all over each other—"

"That is a damned lie," Pres said. "How can you keep a straight face with that stuff spewing out of your mouth?"

Diana shrugged. "Someone had to tell her the truth, that's all I have to say." Then she turned away and lost herself in the boisterous crowd.

Emma stared at Sam, whose face had gone white under her tan. "Sam, you can't possibly believe that . . ."

"I don't know what to believe," Sam said in a flat, dazed voice.

"Come on!" Pres cried. "Do you really have so little faith in me and in your best friend? Sam?"

But Sam didn't answer. She just turned around and walked out the door.

For a moment Emma was too shocked to move, and evidently so was Pres, but finally they ran out after her. She was standing under a streetlight, her head in her hands.

"Sam?" Emma asked, touching Sam's arm.

"Okay, I shouldn't listen to Diana, right?" Sam asked, her voice muffled.

"Right!" Emma cried.

"Girl, you have to have more faith in us than that," Pres said.

Sam lifted her head. "You're right. I do. I really do." She gave Pres a ravaged look. "It would be a lot easier if I didn't care about you so much, you know?"

Pres put out his arms, and Sam moved into them. They stood there under the streetlight, holding each other.

"I'm going," Emma whispered to them softly.

This time no one bothered to protest.

When Emma got back to the Hewitts', she was happy to see that Ethan wasn't downstairs. She went upstairs and into her room, then she threw herself down on her bed and closed her eyes. But she still saw Sam in Pres's arms, and she felt very, very much alone.

"I'm going to call Kurt," she said out loud,

sitting up quickly. She looked at her watch. It was eleven o'clock. *It's not so late,* she thought to herself, *and all this game-playing Kurt is doing is so juvenile.* She scooted over and picked up the phone, quickly dialing the familiar number.

Ring. Ring. Ring.

"Hello?" came a gruff male voice after the fourth ring.

Kurt's father, she realized. *He hates me, I can't ask to speak to Kurt!*

Before Emma could even think about what she was doing, she had hung up the phone.

"Great, Emma," she said out loud, staring at the offending phone that had brought her the voice of Kurt's father. "Now who's the juvenile one?"

SEVEN

"Emma, I can't find Snow White," Katie said, padding into the kitchen the next morning.

Emma added cheese to the omelet she was making. "I'm sure she's around, honey," Emma said absently. She was thinking about Kurt, and whether or not she should try calling him again.

"She *isn't* around," Katie insisted, her hands on her hips.

"Your omelet is almost ready," Emma told the little girl. "Could you please call Ethan?"

"But what about Snow White?" Katie asked, anxiety etched across her face.

"You get Ethan for breakfast and I'll find your kitty for you, okay?"

"Okay," Katie agreed. She stood on tiptoe and peered into the omelet pan. "I don't like cheese in my omelet."

"Yes, you do," Emma said. "I've made it for you this way lots of times."

"Well, I don't like it anymore," Katie said, making a face. "The cheese gets all gunky and slimy."

Emma sighed. "I'll give this omelet to Ethan and make you plain scrambled, okay?"

Katie thought for a moment. "I don't think I like eggs anymore."

I am not in the mood for this, Emma thought to herself. "And why is that?" she asked.

"Well, my friend Julie told me eggs are dead baby chickens."

"That's not true, honey," Emma assured her.

"What are they, then?"

"Chickens lay eggs, you know that," Emma said evasively.

"But if we didn't eat the egg, would it be a baby chicken?" Katie asked logically.

"You eat chicken," Emma pointed out. "It's one of your favorite foods!"

"Not anymore," Katie decided. "I only want toast, okay?"

I give up, Emma thought. *Let Jane and Jeff tackle this one when they wake up.* "Okay," she told Katie. "As long as you eat some fruit with it. Now please go get Ethan."

While the kids were eating, Emma went to look for Snow White. She searched Katie's bedroom, which was where the tiny kitten usually hid out. When she didn't find her, she looked through the rest of the upstairs, then she looked everywhere downstairs. There was no sign of the cat.

"Do you want any more toast?" she asked Katie, coming back into the kitchen.

"Did you find Snow White?" the little girl asked, her mouth smeared with strawberry jam.

"Not yet," Emma admitted. "But I'm sure I will."

Ethan's head jerked up from the comic page of the newspaper. "Your kitten's missing?"

"Not missing," Emma corrected, "we just don't know where she is right now."

"That's what missing means," Ethan replied dryly.

"She's just a tiny little kitten," Emma said, pouring herself a glass of orange juice. "She's probably curled up in a corner somewhere."

"I'm worried," Katie said, her lower lip trembling. "What if she's sick, like Dog?"

"I'm sure she's not sick, honey," Emma assured her. She wet a napkin and wiped Katie's face off.

"You don't know that," Ethan said, sounding even more worried than Katie.

"I know!" Emma exclaimed. "I'll bet she's asleep in your parents' room!"

"Let's go wake up Mom and Dad and see if Snow White is in there," Katie suggested, jumping up.

"No, Katie," Emma said. "They specifically told me they wanted to sleep late this morning. Let's not wake them up."

Ethan's mouth set in an angry line. "Well, I don't think that's right. If Snow White is lost, they'll want to know."

"She's not lost—" Emma began. She looked from Katie to Ethan, and finally gave in. "Okay, go wake your parents."

"You can go," Ethan told his sister, suddenly feigning nonchalance. "I don't even like that cat."

"She doesn't like you, either!" Katie yelled.

"Cats are stupid," Ethan said gruffly. "You can't even walk a cat."

"They are not stupid! You're stupid!"

Emma felt like screaming. *These two are going to drive me crazy today, I just know it,* she thought to herself. "I'll go wake your parents," she told them. "And would the two of you please stop fighting? It's ridiculous!"

Emma marched upstairs and knocked gently on Jane and Jeff's door.

"Yeah?" came Jeff's sleepy voice.

"It's me," she called through the door. "I'm very sorry to wake you, but Katie can't find Snow White and we thought maybe she was in your room."

She could hear Jane and Jeff talking to each other, though she couldn't make out what they were saying.

"I'll look," Jane finally called. "Hold on."

Emma stood there for a couple of minutes, and finally Jane opened the door and peeked her head out. "No cat in here," she told Emma.

"You're sure?" Emma asked. "I can't find her anywhere."

"I'm pretty sure," Jane said, yawning. "We could get up and help you look . . ."

"Oh, no, that's okay," Emma assured her. "Go back to sleep. I'll look again. I'm sure she's somewhere in the house."

Emma found Ethan and Katie standing at the bottom of the stairs anxiously looking up at her.

"Well?" Ethan asked.

"She's not in your parents' room," Emma said, coming down the stairs.

"She's gone!" Katie wailed.

"She's not gone," Emma said with exasperation.

"I want Snow White!" Katie cried.

"Okay, let's approach this in an organized manner," Emma said. "Ethan, you check the entire upstairs again—except your parents' room. Katie, you look in the garage. And I'll check the downstairs."

Emma looked again in every closet and in every corner. She got down on her hands and knees and looked under couches and chairs, all the time calling "Here, Snow White! Here, Snow White!"

Ten minutes later they all met up again in the kitchen. Obviously there was no sign of the cat.

"We should call the police!" Katie cried.

"Don't panic," she told the little girl, smoothing her hair off her face. "We'll go outside around the house. Maybe she somehow got out the front door—"

"She doesn't know her way around yet!" Katie yelped. "She's too little! She's only a baby!"

Emma put her arm around Katie's shoulders and the three of them went outside. She called, "Here, Snow White, here kitty," more times than she could count. They traced every inch of the yard, back and front, but there was no sign of the cat.

"What if a car ran her over?" Katie asked, tears in her eyes.

Emma didn't know what to say to comfort the little girl. This time Ethan put his arm around his little sister. "Come on, Katie," he told her. "Let's go ask the neighbors if anyone saw Snow White."

"You two go over to the Steins'," Emma suggested, "and I'll go over to the Parkses' house." Emma hurried across the yard to the Parkses', where she found a little boy she didn't recognize digging a hole in the front yard.

"Hi," Emma said. "I'm Emma. I live next door."

"I'm Clifford," the little boy said. "I'm visiting my Uncle Craig and Aunt Lisa. I live in California."

"That's nice," Emma said, watching as

the little boy dug deeper into the well-manicured lawn. "What are you doing?"

"Digging for worms," Clifford said, intent at his work. "I'm gonna go fishing."

"I'm looking for our kitten," Emma told him. "Have you by any chance seen a little white kitten?"

"Yeah," Clifford said. He sat back on his haunches. "Don't you guys have any worms here?" he asked with disgust, then he began digging a new hole.

"You did see a white kitten?" Emma asked eagerly.

"I need a whole can of worms and I only got three!" Clifford said. "Man, this stinks."

Emma reached over and pulled the shovel out of Clifford's hand. "Hey!" he yelled.

"Focus for me, here," Emma said. "Now, did you see a white kitten?"

"Yeah, I already told you yeah!"

"When?"

Clifford shrugged. "About maybe a half-hour ago or something."

"And which way did this little white kitten go?" Emma asked.

"It just ran across the lawn here that way," he said, cocking his head in the opposite direction from the Hewitts' house. "Now give me my shovel back!"

Emma handed the boy his shovel. "Thank you, you've been so helpful," she said sweetly. She ran back to the house, meeting up with Katie and Ethan in the front yard.

"No one at the Steins' saw her," Ethan reported.

"I found a little boy over at the Parkses' who said he saw a white kitten half an hour ago," Emma told them.

"Oh, no!" Katie cried, clapping her hand over her mouth. "She *did* get out!"

"It must have been when I went to get the newspaper," Ethan said. He looked miserable.

"It's no one's fault," Emma said quickly. "The important thing now is for us to go try and find her. You two start off on foot that way, and I'll go get the car."

"Come on, Katie," Ethan said, taking his sister's hand.

Emma ran back to the Hewitts' house. Jane and Jeff had just come downstairs.

"Did you find Snow White?" Jane asked, pouring herself a cup of coffee.

"No," Emma said, and she explained what the little boy next door had told her. "I'm going to take the car. The kids are already out looking."

"Maybe we should go out in the other car," Jeff suggested.

"I think we should probably stay here," Jane said. "If Snow White finds her way back, we want to be here to let her into the house."

Just as Emma was grabbing the car keys to the BMW, the phone rang. "Hewitt residence, Emma Cresswell speaking," she answered automatically.

"Hi, it's Kurt," came his voice through the phone.

What timing, Emma thought wearily.

"Listen, about yesterday—" Kurt continued.

"Kurt, I can't talk right now," Emma interrupted him. "Katie's new kitten got out and I have to go search for it."

"Poor kid, she must be so upset," Kurt said.

"She is," Emma agreed. "And I have to go."

"How about if I come over and help you look?" Kurt offered. "I know how much that kitten means to her."

Emma felt her heart swell. "That would be so nice," she said softly.

"Okay, I'll be there in a few minutes," Kurt assured her.

"If I'm not here, I'll be in the car cruising the neighborhood," Emma told him.

"I'll find you," Kurt promised before hanging up.

Slowly Emma cruised down the street, peering out the window, watching for a tiny ball of white fur. She ran into Ethan and Katie two blocks down.

"Anything?" she asked, rolling down the window.

"One kid back there said he saw a cat but

he can't remember if it was white or not," Ethan reported.

"I'm going to drive down the next street, you guys stay on this one," Emma told them. "Oh, Kurt's coming to help us," she added.

"Kurt will find Snow White!" Katie cried. "I know he will!"

She smiled reassuringly at Katie and slowly drove off. *I hope Katie's right,* Emma thought to herself anxiously. *I really do.*

Two hours later they were all sitting in the living room feeling awful. Katie was cuddled up next to her mother, crying, and Ethan was sitting by himself with a scowl on his face.

"Why doesn't everyone just say it's my fault?" Ethan asked in a steely voice.

"Because it isn't anyone's fault," Jane said firmly.

"It is, too," Ethan said. "Snow White had to have gotten out when I went to get the paper this morning."

"Well, even if that's what happened, it

isn't your fault because you didn't see her," Jeff pointed out.

"So?" Ethan shot back. "I should have seen her. I should have been more careful!"

"I want my kitty!" Katie sobbed desolately.

"How about if we make up a flyer?" Kurt suggested. "We could take them around the island and post them all over the place."

"Good idea," Jeff agreed. "And I'll call the *Breakers* and place a lost-kitten ad."

"We'll never f-f-find her!" Katie sobbed. "She's d-d-dead, just like Dog!"

Ethan looked as if he was about to cry, then he jumped up and ran out of the room.

"I don't think she's dead, Katie," Kurt said softly. "We would have found her. I think she's alive and well somewhere, waiting for us."

"That's right," Jane said, rocking the little girl in her arms. "I feel really bad that we didn't have a collar on her with her name and address on it. I sent away for it, but it just hasn't come in the mail yet."

"Snow White is so cute that I'll bet someone found her and just doesn't know where her home is, honey," Jeff told his daughter.

Katie rubbed her red eyes with her fists. "So, what if they won't give her back?"

"I think they will once they see the flyer we're going to make," Kurt replied. "Will you help me?"

Katie nodded yes, and, still sniffling, she moved out of her mother's arms. "What should I do?"

"Can you get me some paper and a Magic Marker?" Kurt asked her.

"Okay," Katie said, and she left the room.

"I think I'll go have a talk with Ethan," Jeff said, getting up. "He's a really sensitive kid. Excuse me."

"I'll go help Katie," Jane said. "Do you guys want tea or anything?"

"No, thanks," Emma said with a warm smile. "I'm supposed to be asking you that."

"We'll take turns, how's that?" Jane asked as she walked out of the room.

"She's great," Kurt said.

Emma nodded. "Thanks for coming over

to help with this. Katie really appreciates it. She thinks you walk on water."

"I just hope we can find her cat," Kurt said. "I lost my cat when I was a kid, and I bawled for days."

"Poor Kurt. I wish I had been there to put my arms around you," Emma said before she stopped to think.

"Do you?" Kurt asked in a low voice.

"Yes," Emma admitted. "I can't stand to think of you being hurt—" She stopped talking. *How can I say that when I'm the one who's hurt him the most?* she realized.

Kurt reached out and touched her hand. "Emma, we need to talk. Yesterday when I told you I was busy last night, I—"

"Okay, I've got the paper and the Magic Marker," Katie said, running back into the family room. "Let's do the flyer really fast and then take it everywhere."

"What should the flyer say?" Kurt asked the little girl solemnly.

"It should say LOST KITTY in really big letters," Katie decided, leaning against Kurt's knee.

"Good beginning," Kurt agreed. He wrote LOST KITTY in big block letters.

"And then it should say her name is Snow White and she's all white and she's really little, and um . . . what else?"

"The area where she was last seen?" Emma suggested.

"Yeah, that's good," Katie agreed. "Oh! I know! One more thing. How about a reward! That way if someone has Snow White and they want to keep her, maybe they'll want money even more!"

"Spoken like the daughter of two lawyers," Kurt said with a laugh. "How much should the reward be?"

"How about ten thousand dollars?" Katie suggested.

"Well, that might be a little high," Emma mused. "How about one hundred dollars?"

"Okay, my mom and dad will pay that," Katie decided. "Put that down."

I'll pay it myself, Emma decided, *and I won't say a word about it.*

Kurt wrote out the flyer, then read it to Katie. "Good?"

"Good," she agreed. "Now we need to make a zillion copies."

"Okay," Kurt said. "Let's go to the zillion-copy-making place."

Katie put her hand trustingly in Kurt's, and turned to look at Emma. "You can come, too, if you want."

"Why, thank you," Emma said with a chuckle. "I would like to come."

They drove to the nearest copy shop and made a hundred flyers, bought some tape and thumb tacks, and then drove to the boardwalk and parked the car in a nearby lot.

"This is pretty far from our house," Katie said as they got out of the car.

"True," Kurt agreed, "but everyone strolls down this boardwalk, so I figure people who live near you might see the flyers here."

"And we can put more up back in our neighborhood," Emma added.

They went from telephone pole to telephone pole, posting the notices.

"I hope it doesn't rain," Katie worried,

staring up at the rapidly gathering clouds. "If it rains the posters will get ruined and we'll have to do the whole thing again."

"I'll go ask if we can put one up in Wheels," Emma offered.

"Okay," Kurt said, "we'll just be farther down the boardwalk."

Emma ran across the boardwalk and walked into the cool air-conditioned motorcycle store. She asked the long-haired guy behind the counter if she could post Katie's flyer.

"Sure," he agreed. "Right in the front window."

Just as she was taping the flyer up, she felt a finger tap her on the shoulder.

"Want to rent a bike, little lady?" Pres drawled, a grin on his face.

"Hi," Emma said. "I'm posting a flyer for Katie Hewitt. She lost her new kitten."

"Poor kid," Pres commiserated. He happened to glance outside and saw Kurt with Katie putting another flyer up on a telephone pole. "You and Kurt work out your problems?"

"That might take a while," Emma allowed. "But he offered to come over and help Katie."

"Cool," Pres said.

"I'm glad I ran into you," Emma said in a low voice. "Actually, I came in here hoping I'd run into you. Were things okay with you and Sam last night?"

"Hard to say," Pres admitted. "She said she was fine, and she knew she should believe us and not Diana, but there was something in her voice . . ."

"That's what I was afraid of," Emma sighed. "And it's so silly! Because we're totally innocent!"

Pres just stared at her, a bemused look on his face.

"Well, we are!" Emma insisted.

Pres held up his palms. "I didn't hear anyone contradicting you."

"If you see Sam, tell her—" Emma began. "Never mind. I'll call her myself."

"Good," Pres said. "It would be a shame to let that evil witch come between your friendship."

"That could never happen," Emma said firmly. "I would never let it. I'll see you later."

Back out in the sunshine, Kurt, Emma, and Katie quickly made their way down the boardwalk. Just as Emma was putting up a flyer on the telephone pole near the Play Café, she heard Kurt whistle.

"What?" Emma asked, securing the flyer.

"I wouldn't believe this if I wasn't seeing it with my own eyes," Kurt murmured.

"You put it up crooked," Katie said, pointing to the flyer.

"That doesn't matter," Emma said absently, and she looked in the direction that Kurt was looking.

And there, sitting at a table outside a burger stand, deep in conversation, were Diana De Witt and Samantha Bridges.

EIGHT

Sam happened to turn her head, and she met Emma's gaze.

"Hi," Emma said, walking over to her friend. She looked over at Diana, then back at Sam, a clear question on her face.

"Hi," Sam replied, her voice sounding guarded and flat. "We were just talking."

"I can see that," Emma said. "I'm just surprised the two of you can find anything to talk *about*." She looked over at Diana again. Diana didn't say a word, she just looked in the other direction.

Very strange, Emma thought. *Something very bizarre is going on here.*

Katie came rushing over to the table. "Sam! My new kitty is lost!"

"Bummer," Sam said, putting her arm around the little girl's waist.

"Yeah, bummer," Katie agreed, imitating Sam. "We're putting up flyers for a reward."

"Smart thinking," Sam told her, nodding solemnly.

"You're lucky you didn't lose Bubba," Katie said.

"You're right," Sam agreed.

Katie frowned. "Do you think Snow White could be visiting Bubba?" she asked hopefully.

"Nope," Sam said. "Bubba isn't allowed to have company. He made a mess of his litter. He's grounded."

Katie smiled. "That's funny." Sam hugged her. "Well, I have to go help Kurt. Bye." She ran off.

"I see you and Aquaman are getting cozy," Diana said, using her nickname for Kurt from when he was swimming instructor at the country club.

"Well, she speaks," Emma marveled. "For a moment I thought you actually weren't going to say anything nasty to me."

"I wouldn't want to disappoint you," Diana said, but the words lacked their usual bite.

"So, do you need help with the flyers?" Sam offered. "I'm free for a couple of hours. The monsters are working at the day camp and Dan is off on a picnic with Kiki."

"You don't have to," Emma said stiffly.

"Hey, I don't mind—" Sam began.

"I can see that you're busy," Emma said pointedly.

Sam looked over at Diana. "We were just talking—"

"You already said that," Emma reminded her. "It's a free country, you know. You can talk to whomever you want."

"Whomever," Diana repeated in a taunting tone. "Don't you just love it when Emma The-Vestal-Virgin Cresswell talks that oh-so-proper talk?"

Emma just stared hard at Sam, silently pleading with her. *How can you be hanging out with Diana De Witt?* she wanted to scream. *How is this possible?* But Sam just looked away.

"Are you mad at me?" Emma asked Sam when she couldn't stand it another moment.

"No," Sam said.

"So, what then?" Emma wondered.

"Nothing," Sam insisted.

Emma sighed. "I have to go. I guess I'll talk to you later." She started to walk away.

"Em!" Sam called to her.

Emma turned around.

"Everything is okay," Sam said.

"If you say so, Sam," Emma said. "If you say so."

"Hi," Kurt said, opening the front door of his house for Emma.

She walked into the coolness of the shabby living room. It had been a long time since she'd been there.

It was late that afternoon. They had spent hours with Katie putting up flyers, then they'd returned to the Hewitts' where there was still no sign of the kitten.

It seemed as if Ethan was the most upset of all, and he kept blaming himself. Emma drove him over to the country club, where he was a counselor-in-training at the day camp, Club Sunset Island, then she'd gone back to the Hewitts' to try and comfort Katie.

After a miserable afternoon, Jane and Jeff and decided to take the kids to Portland to visit friends, to try to get everyone's mind off Snow White. Kurt had invited Emma over, and she'd just arrived.

"Want some lemonade?" Kurt asked.

"Thanks, that would be lovely," Emma said, and winced when she realized she sounded like visiting royalty.

"I take it there's no progress on the lost-kitten front, huh?" Kurt called from the kitchen.

"Nothing," Emma admitted. "The kids are really broken up about it."

"I don't blame them," Kurt said, returning to the living room with two glasses of lemonade. He handed one to Emma.

"Thanks," she said.

"You can sit down, you know," Kurt said. "None of the furniture is booby-trapped."

Emma laughed self-consciously and sat on the frayed couch. Kurt took the oversize chair opposite her. She sipped her lemonade.

"Hungry?" Kurt asked.

"No, not really."

Silence.

"This lemonade is very good," Emma finally said.

"Faith made it from scratch," Kurt explained, referring to one of his two sisters.

"Hmm, well, it really makes a difference."

Kurt jumped up. "This is ridiculous! Listen to us! We sound like two strangers!"

"I guess we feel awkward with each other. . . ."

"Come on," Kurt said. He grabbed Emma's hand and pulled her off the couch, then he led her into the backyard.

It was an unusually hot day, and the sun hit Emma like a furnace.

"How about a dip?" Kurt suggested.

Emma saw there was a small plastic wading pool set up in the backyard.

"What?" Emma laughed. "No high dive?"

"Just take off your sandals, smart-ass," Kurt said, quickly pulling off his sneakers. Together they stepped into the tiny pool. "My dad has had this thing since Faith was a baby," Kurt said. "We have the cutest photos of her in here, wearing a frilly red bathing suit, splashing around. Now it's set up for my cousin Lee Anna's baby."

"So, how many laps of this pool can you swim?" Emma asked.

"Ha-ha," Kurt replied. "I'll race-walk you from one end to the other."

"Oh, sure," Emma laughed.

"Hey, I'm serious!" Kurt said. "Four times back and forth. Loser makes the winner dinner, how's that?"

"Your legs are twice as long as mine!" Emma protested.

"I'll take baby steps," Kurt promised. "On your mark, get set, go!"

Laughing and splashing, the two of them began to walk across the pool. As promised, Kurt took little tiny steps. When they were on the fourth lap, Emma moved into the lead.

"And it's Cresswell in the lead going into the fourth, Cresswell rounding the corner to the finish line," Kurt narrated. "But what's this, folks? Oh, no, Cresswell is down!" He put his foot in Emma's path and tripped her. Squealing, she fell over and plopped into the water, landing hard on her knees.

"You creep!" Emma screamed, laughing so hard she could barely get out the words.

Kurt fell down next to her and splashed her with water. "Oops," he said innocently.

She splashed him in the face. "You did that on purpose."

"Guilty," Kurt agreed.

"This means you're making me dinner," Emma informed him.

"It's a fitting punishment," Kurt agreed.

"I don't have any dry clothes," Emma pointed out, looking down at her white T-shirt and pink and white flowered short-shorts, which were now completely soaked.

"I guess you'll have to go naked," Kurt said innocently.

"I don't think so," Emma said, giving him a look.

"Just a suggestion," Kurt replied quickly. "I'm sure I can find you a garment to put on your lovely back while your clothes dry, madam."

"Thank you, sir." Emma lay back, her head against the inflated side of the pool. She stared up at the fleecy clouds. "Did you ever look at the clouds when you were a kid and see pictures in them?"

Kurt lay back next to her. "Oh, absolutely." He stared into the sky. "See that big one? That looks like a horse."

"It does, kind of," Emma agreed. "And that one over there looks like one of Sam's Samstyles."

Kurt shielded his eyes from the sun with his hand and looked over at Emma. "What was she doing with Diana this afternoon?"

"I don't know," Emma admitted. "I just couldn't believe it when I saw the two of them together."

"They haven't become friends or anything, have they?"

"Not that I know of," Emma replied. "Believe me, Diana is just as awful as she was before you left—maybe worse." *And maybe she's poisoning Sam's mind right this minute about me and Pres,* she thought to herself, *but I'm not about to tell Kurt about that!*

Kurt leaned his head back against the plastic bumper again. "This is nice, huh?"

Emma nodded and leaned back, too, closing her eyes. "Nice," she murmured, enjoying the warmth of the sun on her face.

"Hey, I have a feeling you don't have on waterproof mascara," Kurt said in a low voice.

Emma felt his finger on her cheek, wiping gently. She opened her eyes and looked at the black mascara on his finger. "Do I look like I'm starring in a horror movie?"

"You look beautiful," Kurt murmured. He reached out and touched a wet lock of her hair. "About last night . . . I didn't really have anything planned with my family."

"I didn't think you did," Emma replied.

"Yeah, I'm not the greatest liar. I had fun snorkeling with you yesterday. For a while there I could almost forget everything that happened—it seemed like how it used to be, you know?"

Emma nodded.

"And then it all came rushing back," Kurt continued. "And I thought, 'jeez, Ackerman, what the hell are you doing? What the hell do you want?'"

"What *do* you want?" Emma asked softly.

Kurt sighed. "Yeah, good question. To which I don't have an answer."

"Once you said in your letter that what you dreamed about was . . ." Emma couldn't finish. *You said you dreamed about holding me again,* she wanted to remind him. *You said you didn't think you could live if you didn't. Don't you remember? Don't you?*

"I remember what I wrote," Kurt admitted. "Every word." He didn't make a move toward her.

"Did you change your mind?" Emma asked, half holding her breath.

"No, I didn't," Kurt said.

She turned to him, he looked at her, and then as if she had willed it, his arms went around her until he was holding her against him. It was the most perfect feeling in the world.

"I missed this so much," Emma whispered into his chest.

"Me, too," Kurt said. "It feels like coming home." He pulled away from her just a bit, and ever so softly touched her chin, raising it to him.

Yes, yes, kiss me! Emma wanted to yell. She could feel his breath on her face, her heart was pounding in her chest, and then—

"Kurt? Son? Are you home?"

Kurt jumped away from her as if he'd been burned. Emma recognized the deep voice of Kurt's father. She felt guilty, as if they two of them had been caught doing something illicit.

"Kurt?" Tom Ackerman called again.

"Out here, Dad," Kurt called back. He shrugged at Emma, as if to say "what can I do?"

"We brought the boat in early. Jasper McClean wasn't feeling well," Mr. Ackerman was saying. "I got us some lobster for dinner and—"

Then he saw Emma. And Kurt. Sitting together, soaking wet, in the wading pool. He stared hard at Emma. Then without a word he turned around and walked back into the house.

Emma closed her eyes and wished she could just fly out of the backyard. Kurt's father was a fisherman and a lobsterman, a plain-speaking working-class man who had single-handedly raised his three children after his wife had died of cancer. He hadn't liked Emma much when she and Kurt had first started dating, considering her rich and frivolous. But after he'd gotten to know her better, he had accepted her and finally come to care for her. But he could never, ever forget how Emma had hurt and humiliated his son, and Emma knew it.

"I should just go," Emma said, scrambling up from the pool.

"You don't have to do that—"

"Yes, I do," Emma said, quickly slipping her feet into her sandals. "Your father hates me."

"You're not here with my father," Kurt pointed out.

"Do you remember where I put my purse?"

"It's inside."

"Could you get it for me?"

"Why, so you don't have to run into my dad?"

"Obviously," Emma replied stiffly, pushing some wet hair off her face.

Kurt took her arm. "Emma, whatever decision we make about our future is going to be between you and me. It's not his decision."

"But—"

"But I think that if we have any chance

at all, we have to face him," Kurt said. "Together."

"Oh, God." Emma moaned.

"Come on," Kurt urged. Together they walked into the house.

Kurt's father was getting some lemonade out of the refrigerator. He didn't turn around to look at them or acknowledge them in any way.

"Dad, please don't pretend we're not here," Kurt said.

"I have eyes, I can see who's here," Mr. Ackerman said stiffly. He poured the lemonade and drank it thirstily.

"Emma and I are seeing each other again," Kurt said.

Mr. Ackerman grunted under his breath.

"We're just trying to be friends now," Kurt continued. "I don't know what's going to happen, neither does Emma, but we both agree that we want to spend some time together."

Mr. Ackerman grunted again.

"Look, Dad, I know how much you love me, and I know you want to protect me—"

"You got to live your own life, son," Mr. Ackerman said gruffly.

"Well, that's just what I'm trying to do," Kurt said.

"You don't need me to tell you that girl made a fool of you in front of God and everyone," Kurt's dad added.

Oh, please let me out of here, Emma thought wildly. And she might even have bolted, but Kurt reached for her hand and held it fast.

"Look, Dad, there's a lot of stuff about what went on that you don't know about. I hurt Emma, too." He quickly looked over at her. "I didn't realize then how wrong I was, but I do now."

"You want to be her whipping boy, don't expect me to stand by and applaud," Mr. Ackerman said.

"I don't need your applause," Kurt said. "I don't even need your approval."

"Well, good, boy," Mr. Ackerman replied, setting his lemonade glass on the counter, "because you'll never get it." He looked over at Emma, meeting her eyes for the first time, and the hate Emma saw there made her cringe. "Never," he said again. "You are not welcome in my home."

And Emma was certain he meant it.

NINE

"Emma?" Carrie called from downstairs.

"I'm up here!" Emma yelled down from her bedroom. Then she heard Carrie tread quickly up the stairs.

Good, Emma thought with relief. *I'm so glad she's here. Because I sure do need a dose of Carrie's common sense.*

It was a couple of hours later. Though Kurt had wanted Emma to stay, she couldn't get out of his house fast enough.

"I can't stay where I'm not welcome," she had told him.

"Dad will get over it," Kurt had insisted.

"Kurt, he hates me," Emma replied. "Do you have any idea how that feels?"

"Okay, then let's go out to dinner and talk," Kurt begged.

"I can't right now," Emma replied, on the verge of tears. "I just need some time to be alone." And she fled out to the car.

After driving around aimlessly for a while, she'd gone back to the Hewitts' empty house and tried to sort out her thoughts by writing them down in her diary. That had been no help at all, and finally she picked up the phone and called Carrie, and asked if she could come over.

"No one's home, huh?" Carrie said, coming into Emma's room.

"They're in Portland," Emma replied. Then she explained about Katie's losing Snow White, and how upset both kids were. "We put an ad in the *Breakers* which will start running tomorrow, and we put posters everywhere, so I'm keeping my fingers crossed."

"We should put up some flyers in the Play Café," Carrie suggested. "Everyone goes there."

"Good idea," Emma said listlessly.

Carrie sat cross-legged on the rug. "So why do I have the feeling that you're upset about more than the lost cat?"

"Because you're brilliant and perceptive and you know me so well?" Emma guessed.

"That must be it," Carrie agreed. "What's up?"

"Oh, God, Car, everything is a mess," Emma groaned, throwing her hands over her eyes.

"Let's hear it," Carrie said.

Emma opened her eyes and looked at Carrie with concern. "I just realized—I'm a terrible friend! Here I am about to tell you all my problems, and you're going through torture over Billy!"

"Emma, don't worry about it," Carrie assured her.

"But—"

"I mean it! Besides, maybe hearing someone else's woes will take my mind off my own."

"Okay," Emma relented, "but after my five-minute pity party we give you ten, how's that?"

"Deal!"

"Well, it started today with losing Snow White," Emma related. She told Carrie about the entire day—Kurt coming over to help, seeing Pres, and then the horrible moment with Kurt's father.

"Wow, you sure pack a lot of stress into one day," Carrie marveled.

"It wasn't exactly my idea."

"I know that," Carrie said quickly. She uncrossed her legs and drew her knees up to her chin. "That scene with Mr. Ackerman sounds awful."

"It was," Emma replied glumly. "How can I even consider getting back together with Kurt, when his dad hates me so much?"

"It's not Kurt's father you're in love with," Carrie pointed out.

"But you know how close they are!" Emma exclaimed, nervously plucking at a loose thread in her shorts.

"Look, it's difficult," Carrie allowed, "but it's not impossible. If you and Kurt both want to be together, you can't let his dad stand in your way."

"I tell myself that," Emma murmured, "but then reality sets in. Could you be with a guy your parents absolutely hated?"

"Yes," Carrie said firmly.

"Even if they hated him for a really good reason, like that he'd hurt and humiliated you?"

"I'm telling you, Em, Kurt is a grown-up. His dad will just have to get over it," Carrie maintained.

"What if he never does?"

"I really believe that if things work out for you and Kurt, his dad will come around."

"Well, you have more faith in him than I do," Emma admitted. She pushed some hair behind one ear. "There's also the letter I got from Adam."

Carrie's eyebrows shot up. "Oh, yeah. The letter. I thought he'd decided you were an artistic peon who didn't appreciate his brilliance."

"Read this," Emma said, grabbing the

letter from the drawer of her nightstand and thrusting it at Carrie.

Carrie read it quickly. "Wow, so he really *was* doing speed!"

Emma nodded. "Remember how I said he didn't even sound like himself? Well, now it all begins to make sense!"

"It doesn't change the fact that he hit you up to finance his film," Carrie reminded her.

"I know that. But he believes in it. He thinks it's brilliant. Maybe if I had thought it was brilliant I'd have *wanted* to put up the money."

"I still think it was wrong for him to ask you," Carrie said.

"I do, too," Emma agreed. "But I really care about Adam. And God knows I've done enough stupid things in my life. I don't see how his doing one stupid thing should end our friendship."

"Friendship?" Carrie repeated.

"Okay, it was more than a friendship," Emma allowed. "And I still care about him. I still—" She stopped and threw herself down on her stomach and moaned. "Carrie, I am awful! Terrible! I hate myself!"

"What?"

Emma sat up quickly, leaned over, and grabbed Carrie's hand. "Carrie, promise you won't tell anyone what I'm about to tell you."

"Of course I promise," Carrie said.

"Even Sam."

"You want me to keep a secret from Sam?" Carrie asked dubiously.

"You have to," Emma insisted. "If I don't talk to someone, I'm going to burst."

"Okay," Carrie agreed quietly.

Emma sighed deeply. "Here's the truth of the whole thing. I am still attracted to Adam—"

"What's so awful about that?" Carrie wondered.

"There's more," Emma insisted intensely. "The last few days I've run into Pres a couple of times. We talked, it was great and . . . this is the terrible part . . . I'm really attracted to him! I can't help it!"

Carrie was silent for a moment. "Okay,"

she finally said. "Well, you haven't done anything so awful. Pres is a great guy. It's okay to be attracted to him as long as you don't act on it."

"But something must be the matter with me!" Emma cried. "I mean, I finally realize that I still love Kurt, and at the same time I'm attracted to Adam and Pres! What does that make me?"

"Human!" Carrie said with a laugh.

"Come on," Emma chided Carrie. "You never think of any guy but Billy."

"That isn't true," Carrie said. "Remember Matt Carlton from Paradise Island? And then I ran into him again in New York? I've had dreams about that time I kissed him on the beach. . . ."

"So what are we, hopelessly fickle?" Emma wondered.

"Loving someone doesn't mean you're never attracted to anyone else, you know," Carrie pointed out.

"I don't know anything anymore," Emma said, throwing herself back on the bed. "You haven't heard the worst thing of all.

Sam is jealous of me and Pres. And even though there's nothing going on, I feel guilty because I really am attracted to him . . . and I think he's attracted to me, too."

"Have you talked to Sam?" Carrie asked.

Emma sat up. "What am I supposed to say? I think a lot about kissing Pres, but don't worry, I promise not to actually do it?"

"Maybe," Carrie replied.

"Oh, sure," Emma moaned. "She feels threatened enough as it is. Something very strange is going on with her. Diana tried to tell her that Pres and I were all over each other at the beach—which of course was a total lie. And then today, when we were putting up the flyers, I ran into Sam. And—you're not going to believe this—she was sitting and talking with Diana."

"You're kidding."

"I'm not," Emma insisted. "Do you think Sam could possibly believe the lies that Diana is telling her?"

"God, I hope not."

"What should I do?" Emma wailed.

"Call Sam," Carrie said firmly.

"But—"

"You have to. Emma, Sam is our very best friend. And Diana is the worst kind of poison."

"I know you're right," Emma agreed.

"The only reason you're having trouble calling her is that you feel guilty because you really are attracted to Pres," Carrie said.

"I feel awful about it!" Emma admitted. "But I would never, ever do anything to hurt Sam! I love her!"

"I know you do," Carrie said gently. "Sam knows it, too. This isn't true confessions, you know. You don't have to tell her you're attracted to Pres, or that he's attracted to you. All she needs to know—to feel sure about—is that you would never touch her guy."

But I did once, Emma recalled, full of the deepest regret. *I don't know what I could have been thinking. I can never tell Carrie about that. I can never tell anyone. . . .*

"You know, you and Kurt had problems

because he pushed you too hard, too fast," Carrie mused. "So maybe you're finding yourself attracted to these other guys as a way of protecting yourself against that happening again."

"That makes sense," Emma realized. "That really makes sense." She grinned at Carrie. "Maybe you should consider going into psychology instead of photography."

"No, thanks," Carrie said. "I have no interest in hearing the problems of the entire world."

Suddenly Emma jumped up. "Let's go over to Sam's!"

"I'm game," Carrie agreed, getting up from the rug.

Emma hugged Carrie impetuously. "Thanks."

"I didn't do anything," Carrie protested.

"Oh, Carrie, you don't even know what a good friend you are," Emma said with a fond smile. "Now let's go get Sam!"

"Oh, hi," Sam said when she opened the door to Emma and Carrie. "I didn't expect to see you two."

Bad sign, Emma thought. *She doesn't even sound happy to see us.*

"We just stopped over on the spur of the moment," Emma explained, stepping into the Jacobs's front hall.

"Come on in," Sam said, leading them through the kitchen and into the backyard. "I can't go out because I'm on the night shift with the twins. They're in the family room with some new friend of theirs named Helaina. And trust me, this babe put the hell in Helaina."

Carrie laughed. "You mean she's even more—shall we say—precocious than the twins?"

"Precocious?" Sam echoed ironically. "This girl—who is all of fourteen years old—calmly told me that she gets drunk with her mother at home. They're, like, partying buddies."

"Maybe she exaggerated because she wants you to think she's mature or something," Emma suggested.

"Oh, yeah, I was mondo impressed," Sam replied sarcastically. She sat down on a chair. Clearly this is where she'd been when they'd rung the doorbell. A can of Coke and an open package of Doritos were at her feet. "Anyhow, now she's in there trying to convince the twins they should get a tattoo."

"Mr. Jacobs would kill them," Carrie predicted, sitting on a nearby bench.

"Tell me about it," Sam agreed. "You guys want a Coke or anything?"

"I'm fine," Emma said, sitting in the rocker. She inhaled deeply. "Nice night, huh?"

Sam nodded. "Lots of fireflies."

"So . . . did you have fun today?" Emma wondered.

"It was okay," Sam said, but her face had a closed look on it.

Emma glanced over at Carrie, then back at Sam. "I—I told Carrie I ran into you and Diana on the boardwalk today."

"Uh-huh," Sam said, reaching for the bag of Doritos.

Well, she isn't going to make this easy, Emma thought. "Sam . . . I . . . I was

163

worried," Emma finally said. "I mean, you were with Diana, of all people!"

Sam took a deep swig of her Coke. "I just ran into her."

"But usually when you run into Diana you try to run away from her again!" Emma exclaimed.

Sam shrugged. Emma looked over at Carrie with alarm.

"I think what Emma is saying," Carrie said slowly, "is that we both feel concerned."

"Well, there's nothing to be concerned about," Sam maintained.

"Sam, Diana De Witt is poison," Emma said earnestly. "And she poisons everything and everyone she comes into contact with."

"I'm surprised you guys aren't applauding me for sitting down and having an actual conversation with her," Sam said. "Isn't that the mature thing to do? Rather than having our usual rank-out contest, I mean?"

"But what could you possibly have a

conversation with her *about*?" Emma wondered.

"I can't tell you that," Sam said, and her voice got that closed sound to it again.

It had to have been about me and Pres, Emma thought anxiously. *But how could she listen to Diana?*

"You have a right not to tell us," Carrie said. "But it feels really strange . . ."

"Look, just forget it," Sam said. "Just pretend you never saw us, okay?"

Emma felt worse and worse. "Sam, please, I feel like you're mad at me—"

"I'm not," Sam insisted.

"If it's about me, please, you have to tell me—"

"Did it ever occur to you that it wasn't about you at all?" Sam asked sharply.

"Was it?" Emma asked anxiously.

"Can we just drop this?" Sam said.

"But Diana—" Carrie began.

"Diana what?" Sam interrupted. "She's a person, you know. Not a very nice person, I grant you. Believe it or not, that isn't news to me!"

"Then why were you hanging out with her?" Emma cried.

"I don't want to talk about it," Sam said. "The subject is closed."

Emma felt like crying. "Okay," she finally said in a low voice. "I'll drop it. But . . . please, if you're mad at me, if there's anything you think we need to talk about, promise you'll tell me?"

"Why, do you feel guilty?" Sam asked sharply.

That's exactly how I feel, Emma acknowledged. "I just don't want anything to come between us," she said quietly.

"It won't," Sam promised.

But somehow it seemed to Emma as if Sam couldn't quite look her in the eye. And that hurt most of all.

TEN

"Katie honey, come into the kitchen and eat your breakfast," Emma coaxed the little girl the next morning.

"I'm not moving," Katie said, folding her arms. She was sitting on the couch in the family room, right next to the phone. "I'm gonna sit by the phone until the person calls who stole Snow White!"

Emma went to sit by the little girl and put her arm around her. "We don't know if anyone stole Snow White," Emma reminded her.

"Someone did," Katie maintained. "And she's so pretty they don't want to let her come home to me!"

Ethan came into the family room and sprawled in the easy chair. "That cat is gone forever."

"You don't know that!" Emma said sharply.

"Do so," Ethan said. "Forget it, it's history."

Katie began to cry. "You're mean and I hate you!" she yelled at her brother.

He shrugged and looked away. Katie got up and ran out of the room, crying hysterically. "Mommy!" she sobbed, and ran upstairs.

Emma stared at Ethan, who was busy staring out the window. "You want to talk about what just happened?" she asked him.

"No."

"Well, let's talk about it, anyway," Emma said. "I've never heard you be so cruel before. It isn't like you at all."

"Maybe you don't even know what I'm like," Ethan shot back. "Maybe no one does."

"Maybe," Emma agreed. "So why don't you tell me, then."

"You wouldn't understand," Ethan mumbled.

"Maybe I would. Try me."

Ethan just stared out the window. "Do you know Ian and Becky are breaking up?" he finally said.

What made him bring that up? Emma wondered. "Yes, I heard something about it," she replied.

"Ian really loves Becky, you know?" Ethan said, not looking at Emma. "And she's hurting him bad."

"That happens sometimes," Emma said.

"Yeah, well, it really sucks," Ethan said passionately. Finally he turned to her. "It seems like if you care about something, you just end up getting hurt. Like how I cared about Dog. Like Katie and that stupid cat. Like Ian and Becky. So what's the point of caring about anything?"

Oh, so that's it, Emma realized.

"Sometimes when you care enough, you do get hurt," Emma agreed gently. "But I think that's better than never caring about anything or anyone."

"Well, I don't," Ethan replied. "People who don't care about anything are the lucky ones." He stared out the window again.

"I don't believe that," Emma said.

"No? What about you and Kurt, huh? You guys broke each other's hearts."

"But we're trying again—"

"Just so you can get hurt again?" Ethan interrupted. "Not me. I'm never gonna get caught like that!"

"You care about a lot of people," Emma pointed out. "Your parents, your brother and sister, Dixie—"

"Well, I guess I don't have a choice about my family," Ethan admitted. "But I don't have to care about Dixie. That's a choice."

"You mean you'd end a wonderful relationship with a wonderful person just because you're afraid of being hurt?" Emma asked.

"I can turn it on and I can turn it off," Ethan said in a steely voice. He got up and shook the hair out of his face. "So now I'm turning it off."

"Did it ever occur to you how much that would hurt Dixie?" Emma pointed out.

Ethan just shrugged.

Emma stood up. "I don't believe you'd do that, Ethan. You're a better person than that—more courageous."

"I'm not a better person," Ethan said, his voice trembling. "I'm a terrible person. It's my fault that Katie's cat got out and I know it."

"Ethan—"

"It doesn't matter," Ethan interrupted. "I don't care about anything."

And then he ran out of the room.

Emma sighed. *I wish I knew how to help him,* she thought to herself. *He's a great kid and he's in a lot of pain. He doesn't want to hurt anyone and he doesn't want to be hurt.* She smiled bitterly. *And I know exactly how that feels.*

An hour later Emma was cleaning up the breakfast dishes. She'd finally gotten Katie to eat, but Ethan was a lost cause. She'd just returned from taking Ethan to the country club. Just as she put the last dish in the dishwasher, the phone rang.

"Hewitt residence, Emma speaking," she answered, wiping her hands on the dish towel.

"Hi," came a deep male voice.

"Kurt," she said in a low voice. "Hi."

"How's the search for Snow White going?" he asked.

"So far nothing," Emma said. "Both kids are really upset. Ethan is convinced it's all his fault."

"Poor kid," Kurt commiserated. "I really feel bad for him."

"I know you do."

"So, what did you end up doing last night?" Kurt asked.

"Not much," Emma said.

"I want you to know I had a talk with my dad," Kurt said.

"You didn't have to do that."

"Yes, I did. It was really . . . look, I

don't want to talk about this on the phone. Can you go for a ride or something?"

"Not really," Emma replied. "I'm supposed to take Katie to a friend's house, then I'm running errands this afternoon and making dinner tonight because Jane and Jeff are going to a party."

"What about tomorrow?" Kurt asked. "The owner of Sunset Taxi—you know, the company I used to drive for—asked me if I'd drive some papers over to this guy in Portland tomorrow. Frankly, I need the money. I thought maybe you could come with me."

"What time?"

"Say early afternoon?" Kurt asked.

Ethan will be at camp, Emma thought, *and Jane said something about taking Katie to some mother-daughter thing.* "I think I can go," Emma replied.

"Great," Kurt said. "So if I don't hear differently, I'll plan on picking you up around, say, one o'clock tomorrow, okay?"

"Okay," Emma agreed, and hung up. Almost instantly the phone rang again, and she answered it in her usual proper fashion.

"Hi, it's the guy who deserves a sock in the mouth," came a completely different, deep sexy voice.

"Adam," Emma said, taken aback. "Hi!"

"Hi. Did you get my letter?"

"I did," Emma admitted. "I was happy to hear that good things are happening with your screenplay."

"Thanks," Adam said. "Look, I know in the letter I said I'd wait for you to call me—you can just hang up now if you want to—"

"No, go ahead," Emma replied. She sat down at the kitchen table.

She heard him exhale loudly. "That was my major sigh of relief," Adam said. "I know there's no way my apology can undo what I did . . . but I am so damned sorry."

"So am I," Emma said.

"I messed up a wonderful thing," Adam said earnestly.

"Maybe it's for the best," Emma mused,

wrapping the phone cord pensively around her finger.

"I have a feeling I'm not going to like whatever it is you're about to say."

"Probably not," Emma agreed. "I'm seeing Kurt. We're trying to see if we can work things out."

"Wow," Adam breathed. "That I did not expect. He's back on the island, huh?"

"Yes. He came back to see me."

"So, is that what you want?" Adam asked.

"I don't know," Emma admitted. She bit her lower lip. "I do know that I still have feelings for him; they've never gone away—"

"But he's all wrong for you!" Adam protested. "The two of you have nothing in common!"

Emma stood up and paced nervously with the phone. "Please, don't lecture me on what I want or need, okay? I'll decide that for myself."

"Okay, you're right," Adam agreed. "I was

out of line. I just . . . you're really special to me, Emma. I don't want to lose that."

Emma sighed. "I think you're special, too, Adam. But I . . . I just feel torn in too many different directions right now. I can't give you what you want—"

"I don't think Kurt can give *you* what you want," Adam interrupted.

"Well, it's certainly not your decision to make," Emma pointed out stiffly.

Adam chuckled. "Ouch, I just stuck my foot in my mouth again. I had this all planned out—how I was going to sweep you off your feet over the phone. How when I suggested I wanted to take a trip to the island to see you, you'd say, 'Yes, Adam, it's a wonderful idea' . . ."

"I can't say that," Emma admitted. "Not now."

"You know you're breaking my heart," Adam said, and although his tone was jocular, Emma felt that there might be some truth to it.

I seem to be good at that, Emma thought.

"Adam, we really don't know each other that well—"

"No? I thought we got to know each other really well," he said. "All those hours we spent talking . . ."

And kissing, Emma thought. *I remember that really, really well.*

"I just don't want to lose you," Adam said huskily.

Emma sighed. "I have to tell you the truth about what's going on. Right now Kurt and I are trying to give each other another chance. I don't know what will happen."

"I'm not giving up," Adam warned.

"I really do want us to be friends," Emma said.

Adam laughed harshly. "Emma, that is one tired old line that is unworthy of you."

"So it's either we're a couple or you're out of my life, is that what you're telling me?" Emma challenged him.

"Nope, sweetheart," Adam replied. "I'm saying that I'll be thinking about you. But when you and Kurt crash and burn again, I can't guarantee I'll be around to pick up the pieces."

"I never asked you to do that the last time," Emma reminded him.

"I know that," Adam replied. "But I was glad I did. And I always thought you were, too."

"I was," Emma admitted. "I'll always be grateful to you, and I'll never forget what you did for me."

"I have this terrible feeling we're saying good-bye without really saying it," Adam said sadly.

"I don't know," Emma confessed. "I'm not trying to string you along or play any games. I'm just telling you the truth."

"Yeah," Adam agreed. "And sometimes the truth hurts. Will you write to me sometime?"

"I will," Emma promised.

Adam laughed, but there was a sadness to the sound. "Hey, someday I'm going to be really famous and you're going to regret this decision."

"Maybe I will," Emma said. "Good-bye,

Adam." She hung up the phone and sat there, staring at it. *No one ever told me that love was going to be so difficult,* she thought sadly. *It really isn't like the movies at all.*

ELEVEN

"I thought we'd stop for lunch on the boardwalk before we head over to Portland," Kurt suggested the next afternoon as he pulled his car out of the Hewitts' driveway.

"Do you have time?" Emma asked.

"Sure, I just have to make sure I deliver that packet of papers in Portland today before five," Kurt replied. He glanced quickly over at Emma. "You look great, by the way."

Emma had on a short baby-pink T-shirt that bared her stomach, and baggy gauzy white cotton drawstring pants. "Thanks," she said shyly, then impetuously she put her wrist under his nose. "Sniff me."

"Hmm, it's great," Kurt approved. "Sunset Magic, right?"

"Right," Emma agreed, putting her own wrist up to her nose. "I love it." *And I also feel more comfortable talking about perfume than talking about whatever it is you said to your dad the other evening,* she added to herself.

"So, how is the perfume biz?" Kurt asked as she stopped the car at a red light.

"It's going really well," Emma replied. "We've had to reorder the perfume. The Cheap Boutique has sold out of it three times already."

"So, you're a business mogul now, huh?" Kurt teased.

"I don't know about that," Emma said, "but I'm really enjoying this. Of course it'll be a long time before we actually show any profit, but it looks like there's a chance that we will!"

Kurt looked at her quickly, then looked

back at the road. "And what will you do with this profit if it ever materializes?"

Emma shrugged. "Something to benefit humanity," she intoned portentously, then she laughed at herself. "I don't know, really—give it to charity or something."

Kurt pulled into a parking space off the boardwalk and together they got out of the car. Kurt inhaled deeply. "There's nothing like the air on this island," he said with satisfaction.

Emma laughed. "You always say that."

"So, I'm the poster boy for Sunset Island, what can I tell you?" Kurt said with a boyish grin.

They walked over to the boardwalk. Emma got out her sunglasses and put them on.

"Now you look like a movie star," Kurt told her.

"Of course, because I am a movie star," Emma agreed. "I'm just traveling incognito today so my fans won't mob me."

"Very smart," Kurt agreed, nodding solemnly. "And may I say that last movie you made with Johnny Depp was beyond won-derful?"

"You may," Emma intoned. "Of course, Johnny fell in love with me and I had to break his heart, poor thing. . . ."

Now, why did I say that? Emma thought to herself.

"Well, I can understand why he did," Kurt replied loftily.

Emma looked at him quickly. "I wasn't hinting—"

He touched her hair. "I know that." Kurt threw his arms open, as if he wanted to embrace the entire island. "I don't know about you, you big movie star, but I feel great! Great!"

Emma laughed. *This is the Kurt I used to know—so boyish and enthusiastic.* "Me, too!"

"Hungry?"

"Starved," Emma admitted, and realized it was so.

"How about two chili dogs with every-thing, and extra-large fries and a giant milk shake?"

Emma laughed. "That sounds like a Sam meal!"

Kurt looked away from Emma and stopped in his tracks. "Yup. I guess we could ask her to join us."

"What are you talking about?" Emma asked in confusion.

Kurt cocked his head toward the burger stand. "History is repeating itself."

Emma looked over at the outdoor tables, and there sat Sam and Diana. Again. Only this time they were both dressed in bikinis and they were eating lunch.

"Too weird," Kurt said. "What the hell is Sam doing hanging out with Diana?"

"She won't tell me," Emma said. Suddenly she wasn't hungry at all. "I just can't believe this."

As she watched, Sam leaned over the table and said something to Diana, who nodded her head and then laughed.

It's got to be about me, Emma thought with despair. *Sam must actually believe what Diana's telling her about me and Pres. This is just too awful!*

"You want to take this on or pretend we never saw them?" Kurt asked her.

"I have to say something," Emma decided.

"You don't have to—"

"Please, I'll just be anxious all day if I don't," Emma insisted. She took a deep breath and together she and Kurt walked over to the table where Sam and Diana sat.

"Well, it's the perfect couple out for a stroll," Diana said when she caught sight of them.

Sam looked both embarrassed and defiant. "Hi, whuz up?" she asked, popping a french fry into her mouth.

"We were just going to have lunch," Emma replied, looking with concern at Sam. "What are you doing?"

"Eating," Sam said.

"We spent the morning on the beach," Diana explained, obviously enjoying everyone else's discomfort. She looked over at Kurt. "Hi, there. Nice to see you back."

Kurt nodded coolly. "Nice to be back," he said.

"So, I guess the two of you didn't happen to just run into each other this time," Emma surmised.

"The twins are at camp, so I had the morning free," Sam explained.

That doesn't answer the question as to why you'd spend your free time with Diana! Emma wanted to scream. She took a deep breath. "Sam, could I talk with you a minute? Privately?"

"Okay," Sam agreed, swinging her long legs over the white metal bench.

"Have a seat and tell me what's new," Diana suggested to Kurt.

Emma and Sam walked a few feet away and stood under the shade of a small tree.

"What?" Sam asked, shaking her hair back behind her shoulders.

"What?" Emma echoed. "Sam, what's going on?"

"Nothing," Sam said flatly.

"It's not nothing!" Emma insisted. "You're spending time with Diana!"

"Not too much time, really," Sam replied.

"Any time is too much time!" Emma

cried. "I feel . . . I don't know . . . betrayed!"

"This isn't about you, Emma," Sam stated matter-of-factly.

"I don't believe that!" Emma yelled, then she got hold of herself. "I'm scared. I feel like I'm losing your friendship or something."

"You're not—"

"Sam, Diana hates me. She'd tell any vicious lie about me and then she'd do anything she could to get you to believe it. She doesn't care what she does or who it hurts—"

"Emma, just chill out," Sam said. "Give me a little credit!"

"How can I when I keep running into you with her?"

"Hey, the last I heard I had a mind, you know," Sam replied heatedly. "I'm not some stupid little airhead!"

"Then why are you hanging out with her?"

"I can't tell you that," Sam replied.

Emma threw her hands up in disgust. "Fine. That's just great."

"Emma, really—"

"Just forget it, Sam," Emma said, walking away. She felt truly hurt. "Just forget the whole thing."

"Hey, don't let Sam ruin the afternoon," Kurt said mildly, reaching over to touch Emma's hand.

It was a couple of hours later. They had decided to get back in the car and go to a different part of the island for lunch. Then they'd driven to the ferry, and now they were driving down the street in Portland. Emma had been so upset that she'd barely been able to touch her seafood lunch at a roadside stand.

"I can't help it," Emma said. "I just don't understand it!"

"I don't, either," Kurt admitted. They drove for a few minutes in silence. "I want to tell you about the talk I had with my dad."

"Great," Emma said. "Yet another human who hates me."

"My dad doesn't hate you."

"Oh, you know he does—"

"He doesn't," Kurt insisted. "He told me that himself."

"All right. Does 'intense dislike' ring a bell?" Emma asked. "Does 'You are not welcome in my home' sound familiar?"

"He said it out of anger," Kurt explained. "I'm sure there've been times when you said something out of anger that you didn't really mean."

"I suppose so," Emma admitted reluctantly.

"You have to understand," Kurt continued earnestly, "my dad knew only my side of the story, and my side was pretty one-sided."

Emma looked over at Kurt. "I've done a lot of thinking, Em. I made a lot of mistakes about us. I pushed you too hard and too fast. I was a jerk about your money. And I was so afraid I'd lose you that I almost guilt-tripped you into marrying me. . . ."

"Kurt—"

"No, let me finish while I've got the nerve," Kurt continued. "I told my dad all of that. It was hard for him to hear, you know, because he thinks so much of me. But once I got done feeling sorry for myself, I realized that if I hadn't done all the stupid stuff I did, there never would have been a wedding to walk out on. You weren't ready for marriage. And now I know that neither was I."

Emma looked at Kurt with surprise. "You weren't?"

"No," Kurt replied, taking the car around a sharp curve in the road. "I'm not ready for it now, either. I told my dad that, too. I said that I thought you actually did both of us a favor."

Tears blurred Emma's eyes. "I . . . I can't believe you're saying this—"

"Don't cry," Kurt said with a short laugh. "I'll want to hold you, and that's kind of tough when I'm driving the car."

Emma wiped the tears as they fell down her cheeks. "I just don't know how everything got so mixed up. We both just . . . just lost our way with each other."

"I remember when you first told me about how you wanted to join the Peace Corps," Kurt recalled. "I thought, wow, this girl is so cool. She is really concerned about bigger things than the size of someone's wallet or the latest hip fashion. That's the girl I fell in love with. And then I just got so damned threatened by the idea of you leaving me, I stopped supporting your dreams. . . ."

"You really told your dad all this?" Emma asked.

"Yeah, I did," Kurt replied. "He's a great guy, Emma, really. I know he's quiet and plain-spoken, but he's the most honest, loving man I've ever known. He really listened."

"Did he believe you?"

Kurt chuckled. "He was funny. He put those big hands of his on the knees of his work pants and he said to me, 'Son, why are you telling me this? Seems like you ought to be telling Emma.'"

Emma laughed through her tears. "Did he really?"

"He did," Kurt assured her. "He even said he'd have a talk with some of the people from COPE. And after that to hell with anyone who thought they knew what I should or shouldn't do." He looked over at Emma. "You're crying."

"I can't help it!" Emma cried. "I'm just so happy!" She searched in her purse for a tissue as Kurt pulled the car off the main road onto a side street. "Where are we?" she asked, sniffling back her tears.

"Who cares," Kurt said as he turned off the car. He turned to Emma and held out his arms.

Then, with fresh tears streaming down her face, Emma moved into Kurt's arms, and they circled around her. She cried all the tears she had saved up for so long.

"Your T-shirt is now a disgusting mess," Emma said, pulling away from Kurt slightly.

"That I can live with," he replied, stroking her hair. "But I don't think I could have lived if I had really lost you." Then he touched her chin until she found herself looking into those beautiful blue eyes she had loved for so long, and then his lips were on hers in the tenderest kiss she had ever had.

TWELVE

"Here's the extra marshmallows," Ethan said, handing three bags to Emma.

It was the next evening, and a phone chain around the island had informed everyone there was going to be a huge barbecue in honor of Kristy Powell's new engagement. Kristy's younger cousin Emily, age fourteen, was visiting her, so she had asked that the younger teens on the island be invited, too.

"Thanks," Emma said, setting the marshmallows on the long card table they'd carted out to the beach.

Ethan looked around, his hands deep in

the pockets of his baggy shorts. "Hey, have you seen Dixie?"

"She's playing volleyball with a bunch of kids over there," Emma said, cocking her head a few hundred feet down the beach. "Why don't you go play?"

Ethan shrugged and looked torn.

"Ethan, it's okay for you to care about her," Emma said. "Please believe me. Life is very lonely if you don't allow yourself to care."

"Maybe," Ethan said. He glanced down the beach, where Kurt was helping Jake Fisher and Jay Bailey build a bonfire. "Are things cool again with you and Kurt?"

"It's not as simple as that," Emma admitted, setting out paper cups and paper plates. "But I love him. Even if that means I have to risk being hurt."

"Yeah," Ethan said. "I'll think about it." Then he casually strolled over toward the volleyball game and Dixie.

"Need help?" Carrie asked, coming over to Emma.

"Sure," Emma replied. "You can put out those veggies if you want."

"Wow, something healthy!" Carrie exclaimed. "Whose idea was that?"

"Mine," Emma said. "Kurt and I spent an hour cutting up those things."

Carrie reached idly for a slice of green pepper. "It's good with you two, huh?"

Emma smiled. "Car, I'm so happy! I really feel as if we have a chance. . . ."

Carrie hugged her. "I'm happy you're happy."

Emma pulled away from Carrie and smoothed her friend's hair. "You'll be happy again, too, you know. Billy will come back."

Carrie blinked back some tears. "I miss him so much that it hurts." She reached for another plastic bag of veggies and began to set them up on a plate. "Anyway, I'm trying to stay busy so I won't think about him so much. Of course, it doesn't work very well."

"Maybe you should ask Claudia and Graham if you can have a couple of days off to go to Seattle," Emma suggested.

"I already did," Carrie confessed.

"So what did they say?"

"They said yes. I may go next week." She looked back at Emma. "Then the question is, will it hurt even more to have to leave him than if I don't see him at all?"

"No," Emma said firmly. "When you love someone, you have to risk being hurt. It's the price of admission. I guess I've learned that."

"Great party," Diana said sarcastically, wandering over to them, beer in hand. "Where's Kristy and the new love of her life?"

"I don't know," Emma replied coolly. *Diana doesn't look very good,* Emma thought with surprise. *Her hair doesn't even look combed. I've never seen her look less than perfect in all the years I've known her!*

"Let me tell you something," Diana said, and it seemed to Emma as if she was slightly slurring her words. "Love sucks. Guys suck."

"Thank you for that update on your life," Carrie said lightly. She reached into the bag to get out the hamburger buns and condiments. Diana just turned around and wandered off.

"Now, what was that?" Emma asked Carrie after Diana was out of earshot.

"I have no idea," Carrie said. "But my guess is she's already had a few too many brews."

"We've got the fire going," Kurt said, coming over to them. "Want me to roast you a dog?" he asked Emma.

"Sure," she said absently. She was watching Diana, who had walked over to Sam. The two girls were now deep in conversation. "Would you look at that?" she asked her friends.

"I know," Kurt guessed. "They've decided to join a nunnery together."

Emma hit him playfully in the arm. "It isn't funny."

Kurt put his arm around Emma. "Have a little more faith in Sam, huh?"

"I'm trying," Emma replied. She looked around. "Where's Pres?"

"He's in the volleyball game," Kurt told

her. "Why, you want him to drag Sam away from Diana?"

No, I want Diana to stop telling Sam lies about me and Pres, she thought to herself, but she didn't say a word.

"Here's to Kristy and Greg," Howie Lawrence said, holding his plastic tumbler of Coke up high. "Let's hope this engagement lasts longer than the last engagement!"

"Oooo, rank!" someone yelled, and everyone sitting around the fire cracked up.

It was two hours later. Everyone had stuffed themselves on hamburgers, hot dogs, chips, veggies, watermelon, and marshmallows. The night had grown cooler, and Emma was happily cuddled up next to Kurt. *Now if only I knew what was going on with Sam, I'd be one happy camper,* she thought to herself. But Sam had barely talked with her all day. In fact, it seemed like every time Emma saw Sam, Sam was with Diana!

"Here's to Kurt's return," Darcy Laken

called, holding up her cup. "We all missed you!"

"Hear, hear!" someone yelled.

"I missed you all, too," Kurt said. "And it's great to be back."

"And here's to Billy gettin' his butt back to this island post haste!" Pres called out, hoisting his cup into the air.

Everyone drank to that. Someone turned the portable CD player up, and a Mariah Carey ballad filled the air. Kurt jumped up and reached for Emma. "Dance?"

"I'd love to," she said, and moved into his arms.

"This feels kind of perfect, doesn't it?" Kurt whispered in her ear as they swayed to the music.

"Yes, it does," Emma agreed.

"I know we still have a lot to deal with," Kurt murmured, "but I believe in us, Emma. I believe we can do it. And I believe it's worth the risk."

"Me, too," Emma said, holding him close. She stood on tiptoe and kissed him softly, her arms draped around his neck.

"Oh, real cute," a loud voice boomed nastily, practically in Emma's ear.

It was Diana, and she looked even worse now than she had before. She had a beer in one hand and a cigarette in the other.

"You're drunk," Emma realized.

"Well, aren't you the mental giant," Diana slurred. "So I see you and Aquaman are all huggy again, huh?"

"Diana, go get some black coffee or something," Kurt suggested. He held Emma close, and the two of them swayed to the music.

"He's not so great, you know," Diana told Emma, ignoring Kurt. "And I should know, know what I mean?"

"Go to hell," Emma said flatly. She stopped dancing and faced Diana.

"Ooo, tough talk from the perfect girl. Well, I'm *so* shocked," Diana taunted.

Sam padded over to them through the sand. "Diana, cut it out," she said in a low voice.

"Don't tell me what to do," Diana said. She pushed some hair off her face. "Hey, do you think Emma Cresswell wears an actual chastity belt?" she asked. "You know, so no one can get to her private parts? Of course, that would assume that perfect Emma Cresswell even *has* private parts!"

"Diana, you're drunk and obnoxious—" Kurt began.

"Says who?" Diana challenged him belligerently.

"Diana—" Sam began, reaching for Diana's arm.

Diana just shook her off. "I don't have to listen to you!" The music stopped, and suddenly Diana's voice seemed so loud that all other conversation stopped. "I don't have to listen to any of you because you all suck!"

"I give up," Sam said with disgust.

"Poor you," Diana said, almost falling over in the sand. "Why should I feel sorry for you? You're doing fine. I'm the one who's pregnant!"

A hush fell over the crowd. There was no sound but the crackle of the fire.

"Come on, Diana," Sam finally said,

reaching for Diana again. "I'll take you to get some air—"

"I'm out in the air, you stupid idiot!" Diana yelled, waving her arms wildly. She looked around at everyone. "So, what's everyone staring at? I'm pregnant! Isn't that a hoot! Isn't that the funniest thing you ever heard?" Just then Diana's face turned green in the firelight. "Oh, God, I'm going to be sick—" She staggered down the beach making wretching noises. Sam ran after her.

"Wow," Carrie said, standing close to Emma.

"She's pregnant?" Emma said with shock. "I can't believe it!"

"How could it have happened?" Carrie asked.

Kurt shot her a look.

"I'm not stupid, I know how it happened," Carrie said, dryly, "what I meant was how could she have *let* it happen?"

"Accidents happen," Emma said faintly. Because the moon was full, she could just make out Diana's figure in the distance.

She was hunched over, and Sam was with her.

"She must be crazy," Emma said. "She's drinking and smoking—"

"Emma, if Diana is pregnant, that means she could actually be a mother," Carrie pointed out.

Emma shook her head. "Scary."

Kurt put his arm around her. "Diana is an accident looking for a place to happen."

"But what if she did have the baby?" Emma protested. "She can wreck her own life if she wants to, but she doesn't have the right to wreck someone else's!"

Sam left Diana and walked slowly over to Emma, Carrie, and Kurt. "She wants to be alone," Sam said.

Kurt kissed Emma on the cheek. "I think I'll leave the three of you to talk like the good guy that I am."

"You knew?" Emma asked Sam.

Sam nodded. "The other day when I ran into Diana on the boardwalk she told me she thought she was pregnant. Lorell just left for California and she didn't have anyone to talk to."

"So she picked you?" Carrie asked incredulously.

"Yeah, kinda weird, huh?" Sam admitted. "But I guess she figures I mess up so much I wouldn't judge her for messing up—something like that."

"And that's what the two of you have been talking about all this time?" Emma asked incredulously.

Sam nodded. "She asked me to promise not to tell anyone, and I promised. That's why I couldn't tell you about it. I mean, I can keep a secret, you know—even Diana's."

Emma flushed with remorse. "Sam, I am so sorry—"

"Forget it!" Sam said. "It's no biggie."

"But it is," Emma insisted. "I was so sure that Diana had convinced you something was going on between me and Pres—"

"If she hadn't been so wrapped up in her own misery, she probably would have tried," Sam admitted. She dug her sandal into the sand. "I couldn't just turn my back on her, you know? It was funny in a way. I mean, I still can't stand her, but I feel kind of sorry for her, know what I mean?"

Emma nodded. "So is she certain that she's pregnant?"

"I told her to go take one of those home pregnancy tests, but she hasn't done it yet," Sam said. She shook her head ruefully. "And if she is pregnant, she doesn't even know who the father is!"

"That is terrible," Carrie said.

"Tell me about it," Sam agreed. She laughed. "Listen, the only good thing about spending any time with Diana is that I seem totally sane by comparison!"

As if on cue, the three of them began to walk slowly toward the ocean.

"You know, I was jealous of you and Pres," Sam admitted, looking out at the ocean. "I can't deny it. And I suppose I was purposely vague when you asked me what was going on with Diana because of that."

"I would never—" Emma began.

"I know that," Sam interrupted. "Believe

me, I know what a great person you are. Can I help it if insecurity is my middle name?"

"Pres loves you," Carrie reminded Sam.

"Yeah, I know that, too," Sam said. "Well, sometimes I know that." She sighed. "How do you get confident about a guy, that's what I want to know!"

"That's what we *all* want to know," Carrie said with a laugh.

"It's just that if you really, really care, you can really, really be hurt, you know?" Sam asked plaintively.

Emma looked over her shoulder and saw Kurt standing near the fire with Jay, Jake, and Erin. Her heart was filled with love. "It's worth it," she said passionately.

"You just feel that way right now because things are good for you and Kurt," Sam pointed out. "You didn't feel that way when you were miserable!"

Emma shivered and pulled her jacket closer around her. "No, I guess I didn't. But it seems as if that particular lesson has been all around me lately. So maybe I'm finally learning it."

Just then Emma heard Kurt exclaim loudly, followed by excited voices, laughter, and shrieking.

"I wonder what that's all about," Carrie said.

The three of them hurried over to the campfire, where they found Kurt holding a tiny, shivering white bundle of fur. "It's Snow White!" Kurt exclaimed. "I looked down and there was this little white thing chewing the remains of someone's burger!"

"Oh, my God, I don't believe it!" Emma cried. She held out her hands for the kitten and snuggled it to her. "Where did you come from?" she wondered. She looked around and saw Ethan making his way through the crowd. "Look!" she marveled.

Ethan took the kitten into his arms. He looked as happy as Emma had ever seen him. "Katie will be so happy!" He nuzzled his face against the kitten. "How did you get here, huh?"

"I'm a sucker for a happy ending," Sam sighed.

Pres came up and put his arm around her. "Me, too," he told her, kissing her on the neck.

Ethan looked at Emma, his face beaming in the firelight. "I lied, Emma," he said. "I really do like this kitten."

"I knew that," Emma replied gently.

Shyly Ethan reached for Dixie's hand, and still holding the kitten, they walked away together down the beach.

"That's one great kid," Kurt said, his arm around Emma's shoulders. "I'd like to have a son like him someday."

Emma gave him a look. "Someday in the far, far distant future," she said distinctly.

"Yeah," Kurt agreed with a laugh. "The far, far distant future. For right now I just want to concentrate on you."

"It's a deal," Emma agreed. She wrapped her arms around his neck. "I missed you so much. I know it won't be easy, but—"

"But it'll be worth it," Kurt finished for her. "I believe that with all my heart."

And then he sealed it with a kiss, and Emma knew he meant every word.

"Love is worth everything, don't you think?" Emma whispered to him.

"I'm not thinking at all right now," Kurt said, "and neither should you." Then he picked her up in his arms and carried her away from the crowd, until they were lost in a world all their own.

SUNSET ISLAND MAILBOX

Dear Readers,

Ah, love. Writing about the continuing romantic adventures of Emma, Sam, and Carrie really takes me back to what I went through at that age. Torture! And bliss! And then torture again! Some people say that you never forget your first love, so I tried to think . . . just who <u>was</u> my first love? And you know, it's funny, but what I thought was love then and what I know is love now are two very different things. I mean, when I was younger and dumber I had relationships where I lived and breathed for the guy—and we all know how stupid that is, don't we! Sure, but knowing doesn't always stop us from doing it, right? Oh well, we live and learn!

And speaking of living and learning . . . I recently received a poignant letter signed only "Jennifer, Somewhere in New Jersey." Now, usually I never print letters without a name and address, but I want to share a little of this one with you.

"Hi. My name is Jennifer. I'm writing in response to the girl who wrote about getting pregnant at age seventeen in the back of Sunset Heart. *I just had a baby, and I wish I had waited. I had so many dreams. I wanted to become an elementary school teacher but now I can't. My boyfriend and I got married even before I knew I was pregnant, but all the fun things in our life are put on hold. If you get pregnant life changes practically overnight. I love my baby but I wish with all my heart I had waited. I'm not signing my name because I plan to save all*

your books for my little girl to read some day, and I wouldn't want her to get the wrong idea. Thanks, Cherie, your books mean so much to me . . ."

Pretty powerful, huh? Sometimes I think girls fall in love with the fantasy of having a baby. Or they believe it will make a guy stay with them. If I could walk up to every single one of you and convince you how wrong this thinking is, I would do it. You are too smart, too cool, and have too much going for you to buy into those lies.

I think the world of all of you. I guess I don't need to tell you by now that I answer each and every letter I get. As my great pal Lisa Hurley in Long Beach, California, says, You guys kick butt!

See you on the island!
Best-
Cherie Bennett

Cherie Bennett
c/o General Licensing Company
24 West 25th Street
New York, New York 10010.

Dear Cherie,
I just got finished reading Sunset Stranger *and it was great! I think that a book from a guy's point of*

view would be great. I think it would be cool if it was coming from Pres's point of view and have it be about how he feels about Sam.

> *Love always,*
> *Kristen Johnson*
> *Bremerton, Washington*

Dear Kristen,

I've gotten about a dozen letters lately about doing a book from a guy's point of view. Everyone suggests a different guy! Some say Billy, some say Pres, some say Kurt, someone even suggested Graham Perry, even though he's quite a bit older! So what do the rest of you out there think? I'd love to know!

> Best,
> Cherie

Dear Cherie,

Hi, my name is Tarra Nolan. I'm fifteen and I've been reading your books for about two and half years. I read them as soon as they come out in the bookstore. It's weird but I really feel as if I know Sam, Carrie, and Emma in real life. I would be so upset if you ever stopped writing these books. You asked in one book about kids drinking. Well, I wanted to say that I've never been drunk in my life, but there are a lot of kids who choose to do stupid stuff like that.

> *Your faithful reader,*
> *Tarra Nolan*
> *Bay City, Michigan*

Dear Tarra,

I've gotten a lot of mail in response to my question about drinking. You all may remember I asked if any of you out there drink alone. Well, the answer was yes, some of you do. And every letter I received from a person who was honest enough to admit this said she felt really bad about it. Every single girl said she did it because she was unhappy and it seemed to make her feel better for the moment. I do appreciate the honesty of all who wrote about this. And I can truly understand being that unhappy. I, for one, hated many things about being a teenager, though I didn't drink. So now the question is, rather than continue to act out in this fashion, what can you guys do to change? Any ideas out there? I know you all care about the Sunset Sisterhood, so let's see if we can get an honest dialogue going on this!

> Best,
> Cherie

Dear Cherie,

I never really liked reading until I read Sunset Dreams. *Now I can't put your books down even to do homework! The stories are so real! What advice would you give a reader who was in Sam's shoes (or should I say cowboy boots?) in* Sunset Touch?

> *Your greatest fan,*
> *Lacey Wilson*
> *Bethel Park, Pennsylvania*

Dear Lacey,

I love your name, by the way! I would give Sam the same advice Carrie gives her—if you really love a guy, you can not play games with him. It never works. I realize this advice is easy to give and hard to follow! But as the girls all discuss in this book, love is worth the risk!

> Best,
> Cherie